THE
TIDES
OF OUR
SINS

AMY TACKETT

Cover Design by Mel D. Designs

Edits by Ozor Edits

Printed in the United States of America

ISBN 979-8-9886589-2-4 (Paperback)

Official Playlist

Songs to pair with your reading experience:

"If I Die Young" — The Band Perry
"Island in the Sun" — Weezer
"Summertime Sadness" — Lana Del Ray
"Easy on Me" — Adele
"Riptide" — Vance Joy
"This Is No Burial" — Andie Elise
"Down to the River to Pray" — Alison Krauss
"Banana Pancakes" — Jack Johnson
"Rich Men North of Richmond" — Oliver Anthony
"Unwritten" — Natasha Bedingfield
"Rescue" — Lauren Daigle
"Jamming" — Bob Marley
"A Drop in the Ocean" — Ron Pope
"Young and Beautiful" — Lana Del Ray
"Praying" — Kesha
"Here Comes the Sun" — The Beatles
"Clean" — Taylor Swift

"If you declare with your mouth, 'Jesus is Lord,' and believe in your heart that God raised him from the dead, you will be saved."

—Romans 10:9

EMILIA
NOW

EMILIA ALWAYS KNEW SHE would die young.

She'd felt it in the marrow of her bones, even from the ripe age of five when she would awaken from a nightmare screaming for her papà as visions of hellfire and brimstone all but consumed her. Of course, Emilia couldn't yet verbalize the feeling, the sense of knowing, until she was much older.

But she knew, all the same.

What she didn't know, though, was that it would be by her own hand.

She would be her own undoing.

She scuffed at the rocks under her feet, then curled her bare toes inward, burying them into the dirt. It was late May, and she stood atop a cliff at the edge of her family's vineyard in Cape Cod. Somewhere in the distance, a seagull squawked, and the tides beneath her were lapping angrily against the shoreline, as if they, too, could sense her arrival. She inhaled the warm, salty sea breeze as it rose and stung her nostrils.

It really was a beautiful day to die.

Emilia sighed, reflecting on the many years she'd spent fixated on the departure process. She'd researched so many questions, but a simple internet search couldn't answer some things. Things like whether she'd feel warm or cold as her body passed from one life to another. Whether death would happen instantaneously or if she'd float away, hovering over the cusp of Earth as she waved goodbye to all she'd ever known.

She could never voice these concerns, though. Questions about death were never well received.

Her parents had raised her in the church. As Italians, they'd been devoted Catholics, and as a wife, Emilia had attended several Protestant churches with her husband, Nick. But she had never fully known if she believed in God. The Bible and the concept of Jesus were so complex, so infinite in a way her finite mind could not comprehend, that it was impossible for her to know if it was all real. To simply accept the stories and their origins and *believe without seeing*, as people in the church liked to say.

How Christians so rigidly believed in one way when there were so many other rationales was beyond her. If everything in the Bible was real, for example, and she jumped off this cliff today, taking her own life, would she be obliterated in the depths of hell, as the Bible implies? Or would God have mercy on her? Would he realize she wasn't in control of her actions anymore? That something else, something dark and sinister, had wrapped itself around Emilia's prefrontal cortex long ago, slithering through her mind like a cobra, slowly squeezing the life out of her with each passing breath.

Tears sprang from behind her lashes at the thought, and she sat, crossing her legs.

She didn't want this.

She hadn't wanted any of it.

What are you waiting for?

Squeezing her eyes shut, she rubbed her face and tossed her long, billowy hair from one side to the other, letting her midnight-colored locks dance in the wind as she tried desperately to block out the compulsive thoughts. The sudden eruption that had eroded her life had been more devastating than she could ever imagine. It'd been eleven months to the day since her world split in two, since the tectonic plates of her heart had shifted, never to be mended again but rather to be made into something new.

Except she didn't want something new.

She wanted her old life—the one where she was happy and carefree, a loving wife and mother to three. She wanted to return to her previous reality, where grape harvests and tourism numbers were her biggest concerns, not to this new universe in which she existed.

She wanted another option besides pain or numbness.

In the distance, a boat sped by, sending a new ripple of waves through the waters. Emilia's spine straightened at the sight, not wanting to draw attention to herself.

If you don't want anyone to see, then get on with it.

The words hissed in her mind, only they weren't her own.

Just jump, Emilia. Give your daughters this one gift.

More tears broke through her vision now, and she stood.

She stood, and she stared at the waters, thinking about the logistics of it all once again, only this time, from a pragmatic perspective. What would happen to the business? How long would it take for them to find her? *Would* they even find her, or would her body be lost at sea, never to be seen again? Or perhaps her corpse would wash up on shore outside the lighthouse a decade from now, finally giving her son the sense of closure he didn't know he needed.

At that last thought, she bit the inside of her cheek, wincing when the taste of iron hit her tongue.

Luca.

Her little boy. He didn't deserve to grow up like this.

None of them did.

Turning from the cliff's edge, she slipped her sandals back on and faced her office on the opposite side of the vineyard. If she was going to jump and leave her only son without a mother, then she needed to give Nick instructions. Nick was a great father, but certain things required a mother's touch, a mother's love.

Someone who would tell him it's okay for boys to cry, too, and that picking on the girl you like isn't actually the way to her heart. What to say to Luca when he has his first heartbreak, how to coach him through the situation if he's the one doing the heartbreaking. Her son needed a father who could play both mommy and daddy, and Emilia had to ensure Nick was equipped.

Still in a fog-like trance, she brushed the messy black curls from her face and set off down the vineyard's long path, determined to leave the thumbprint of her heart somewhere in the loose-leaf pages she was about to grab.

EMILIA

THEN

"LUELLA, BE NICE TO your little brother."

Luella rolled her eyes and audibly groaned from across the kitchen island. "*Mammone.*" The word came out under her breath but was still loud enough for Emilia to hear.

Mommy's boy.

"I'm serious," Emilia warned, pointing a spatula at one of her sixteen-year-old twin daughters. "You and your sister need to be good role models for Luca. He's only five. He looks up to you two."

Luca crammed another piece of bacon in his mouth and promptly stuck his tongue out. "Yeah!"

"*Oh mio Dio,*" Emilia mumbled as the kids continued to bicker. "Just be nice to each other, please. I'm already under enough stress without you all fighting all day, too."

It was only nine in the morning and already Luella and her twin sister, Tallulah, had had a screaming match over a missing orange lip gloss. Emilia wasn't in the mood for a second uproar this early in the morning.

"Do we have to go tonight?" Tallulah asked, talking around a bite of scrambled egg.

"Yeah, can we skip it?" Luella whined.

Emilia looked at her children in shock. Of course her kids needed to be there. Tonight was the annual summer solstice celebration at the winery, and the Davenports always attended as a family. As a partial owner with her brother, Cassio, Emilia took immense pride in the family business. Her parents had opened the winery thirty-some-odd years ago after uprooting the whole family from Italy to come to America. They'd had a good run for a few decades, but then Emilia's father, Leonardo, got sick. The doctors diagnosed him with stage-four terminal lung cancer, and it wasn't long before Emilia had to say goodbye to her papà.

Her mamma, Isabella, died a year later from a stroke.

"No, you cannot skip it," she said through gritted teeth before going back to flipping pancakes. "This is our winery now, our family's business. It's what pays for your education, this house, this food, all your fancy clothes. If you all want to continue having nice things, then you will respect Fiore Vineyards and appreciate all it has given us."

She poured the last of the batter onto the griddle and took a deep breath, readying herself for more arguing. Luckily, she didn't have to.

"Good morning, my beautiful family!"

Her husband came bounding into the room, immediately soaking up their kids' attention. Some days, she was jealous of how easily they all gravitated to him, the same way flowers naturally drew to light. Nick, with his golden-blond hair and lopsided, boyish grin, may as well have been the damn sun, while Emilia was the moon. She had long hair that was dark as night and a cool, calm exterior that tended to lull people rather than excite them in the way her husband did.

Today, though, she was grateful for it.

"Daddy!" Luca jumped down from his stool and ran to Nick, wrapping his arms around his thighs.

"Hey, buddy," Nick said, brushing his son's sandy-blond hair out of his face. "Are you guys ready for tonight?"

Emilia watched as Tallulah and Luella exchanged a quick glance, both with their arms crossed tight over their chests.

Nick saw it, too, and arched an eyebrow.

"Sure, yes, we're excited," Tallulah finally said. "But I'm counting it toward my community service hours when I apply for college."

Luella rolled her eyes, and the action made Emilia smirk. Her girls were so different despite their identical appearance.

"I will be hanging out with Chad Farber, aptly not volunteering," Luella said.

"Ugh," Nick groaned. "Must you talk to boys? Can't you just never date like your sister?"

Tallulah's cheeks colored while Emilia's smirk blossomed into a full-blown laugh.

"Okay, okay, enough," Emilia said, intervening before the bickering had a chance to resume. "Finish up your breakfast, please. We have a lot to do before the party tonight, and I'd like everyone to arrive unscathed."

Her children all promptly stuck their tongues out at each other while Nick ruffled Tallulah's hair and elbowed the other two. Emilia shook her head and refilled their plates, loving the symphonious chaos of her family.

"EXCUSE ME, BUT THAT isn't supposed to go there!" Emilia yelled at Jacob, the musician she'd hired for tonight. They were only an hour away from the event's start time, and her anxiety was harsher than the tides. "Please, I said to set up under the tent canopy."

The man mumbled an apology, and she nodded, shooing him off. She'd originally booked Stacey Springer, a singer who'd been to the winery several times over the years, but she'd canceled at the last minute, apparently going into labor. Emilia didn't even know she was pregnant, and although she was frustrated, she'd understood. Her daughters had come early, too—a scary, beautiful situation that was no one's fault.

The extent of her empathy ended when she met Jacob. He'd arrived twenty minutes late, smelled like cannabis, and had a mustard stain on his denim jacket.

"Remind me not to hire anyone from Facebook Marketplace again," she said to her assistant manager, Zoey.

"What?" she asked, stifling a laugh. "You telling me you never smoked?"

Emilia gave her a look, suggesting no such thing. "You're hilarious."

Zoey snickered to herself, then went back to checking items off her clipboard. "So I just checked in with Sal, and the food truck is all set up and ready to go. They're doing a limited menu to complement the new lavender wine." She paused, flipping a page over and tapping her pen as she inspected her writing. "I wrote down citrus salad, grilled halibut, and a creamy goat cheese platter with honey and herbs."

Emilia nodded as she took deep breaths, trying to calm her irritated nerves. "Excellent. And the sparklers?"

"All set." Zoey clicked her pen and tucked it behind an ear, showing off her black spiral curls in the process. "The bonfire is also ready to go, as well as the yard games for the kids."

Her face curled into a gentle smile, and Emilia's heart warmed. She'd been skeptical about them hiring Zoey when her brother first brought her on. She was a recent graduate with no prior experience, and truth be told, Emilia suspected Cassio only hired her for her looks. At five feet seven with a slim waist and ebony skin, she was beautiful, but Emilia had been pleased to find she was more than just a pretty face. Zoey was an excellent project manager, and the guests all loved her. Emilia would need to increase her pay soon if she didn't want to lose her to the competition.

"*Grazie*, Zoey." Emilia smiled in return, then reached for the clipboard. "Here, go take your break before the crowd gets here. I can handle the rest."

Zoey quickly obliged, waving as she ran back to the office. Biting the inside of her cheek, Emilia scanned the list again, sighed, and then decided to head to the bar. She'd already tried the new wine a dozen times, but once more couldn't hurt. They were debuting a limited edition summer wine called *Lavanda Blanc*, which was a lavender-infused white wine she'd come up with on her own. Before her parents passed, they'd only ever made and sold three staples: a red blend, a chardonnay, and a rosé. When she and Cassio took over, they'd agreed to try new products in light of the mountain of debt their parents had left them with.

The inheritance—if that's what you could call it—had come as a shock. The business had always been viable, a popular spot for locals and tourists alike; she'd never suspected they'd actually been throwing money into it like a sinking ship.

We should sell it, she remembered telling Cassio when they first found the financial statements. *Sell it all off and cut our losses. Let someone else handle the problem.*

But her brother hadn't been receptive, not in the least.

You want to sell Mamma and Papà's legacy? His words had been so vindictive, so full of acid. *I won't have it.*

Emilia had tried to reason with him, but it was pointless. In the end, she'd submitted to his wishes, agreeing to help run the company until they'd gotten out of debt. Then, they'd reevaluate to see if it made sense for Cassio to buy out her shares.

"One glass, please." She raised a single finger at the bartender, who quickly fulfilled her request. Smiling, she thanked him and sat on one of the end stools, swiveling around to stare at the lush vines that draped the grounds. Normally, they were just ordinary rows of grapes you'd expect to see at any vineyard, but Zoey had convinced her to invest in twinkling lights to weave through the vines for tonight's celebration. It was only 6:00 p.m., but already, Emilia could tell the party was going to be beautiful, unlike anything she'd ever seen on the grounds.

She sighed and took a sip of her drink, the euphoric scent of lavender hitting her nose before the citrus flavors burst in her mouth. Her taste buds danced and swayed before the acidic shock mellowed into a more subtle, herbal taste, hints of basil and thyme soothing her palate.

It was perfect.

Which means tonight would be perfect.

She took another deep breath, followed by a second sip. It's not that she'd actually wanted to sell this place, nor did she know if she wanted to give her brother her shares. Emilia loved the vineyard. It was a beautiful piece of property filled with so many lovely memories. Her papà chasing her around the grounds as a child, her mamma taking her out to the edge of the cliff near the sea for secret picnics, the many faces she'd met over the years as travelers stopped by. It had been a magical place to grow up, a unique childhood existence she wouldn't trade for the world.

The problem, though, was ownership often brushed away that magic. She'd gotten a glimpse of it when she'd worked here under her parents' authority, but they'd hidden the broken parts under a facade, doing everything in their power to keep the magic alive, the way parents often do.

And just like children often do, Emilia had realized the truth too late, and her world was turned upside down the moment she stepped into this position. Cassio had volunteered to take over the accounting side of things, seeing as that's what he went to school for and he could do it remotely from his home in Italy, but even with that stressor off her plate, she still knew the fate of the business landed on her. Cassio may be the brains, the traditionalist, the one keeping her grounded in this new reality, but Emilia was the visionary. This night, this wine, had all been her idea, just like so many others. Revitalizing the business so that it would bring in enough revenue to fix its insurmountable debt was a task she'd spearheaded and would continue to lead until they were in the black—something she was not looking forward to chatting with Cassio about during his visit tonight.

A tension headache pulsed at the thought, and Emilia tipped up her glass, downing the rest of her wine before replacing it with more.

"How 'bout another round of applause for Cassio, Emilia, and Emilia's beautiful family?"

The audience cheered as Emilia and her crew waved, making their gracious exit from the small, makeshift stage. Despite her earlier fears, the night had gone off without a hitch, at least so far. They'd sold over one hundred tickets at the door, the food and drinks had been flowing effortlessly all night, and the audience had loved Jacob's acoustic set. Emilia might've even tapped her foot a time or two, smiling and feeling guilty for judging him.

"Emmy," Cassio said, interrupting her thoughts and grabbing her elbow. "Come, sit, eat." He flashed his white, charismatic smile. "You haven't stopped all night. Come soak it in; enjoy the night."

She chewed the inside of her lip, torn between heeding her brother's advice and running off to check the sparkler-bonfire situation. Zoey had assured her it was safe, but she couldn't help the sinking feeling in her stomach that said it was a wildfire waiting to happen.

"Come, *amore mio*," Nick said, kissing her cheek. "The kids haven't eaten either. Let's have a meal together."

Emilia scanned her husband's tousled blond locks, then his incandescent grin, and smiled, tucking her lips in. She loved nothing more than when he spoke to her in her native language.

"Fine, yes," she said, reluctantly letting the two men lead her toward a table in the back. "I suppose I do need to soak up some of this wine."

"*Lavanda Blanc*!" Cassio boomed, the accent thick on his tongue. "What a delicious wine." He paused, pulling out Emilia's chair for her while Nick ran off to pick up the food. "Mamma and Papà would be so proud of you, Emmy."

Emilia felt a blush creep up her neck until it stained her cheeks. It had always been hard for her to accept compliments. "Thank you, Cass. They would be proud of you, too." She squeezed her little brother's hand, then turned her attention to the crowd around her.

In all her years, she'd never seen the vineyard this full of people, this happy, this full of life. Smiling guests overflowed the tables while others toured the vines under the glow of the twinkle lights. She shifted her gaze to the lavender fields just beyond the grapes, where children were running with sparklers while their parents observed from the comfort of their wooden chairs near the fire. It really was a perfect night.

Maybe this can work, she thought as a warm ocean breeze blew by. *Maybe we can still save the vineyard.*

"Alright, I've got a little bit of everything." She rotated her body back toward the table at the sound of her husband's voice. "Luca, I know you want french fries, but just humor me and try one bite of everything. If you don't like it, we'll pick up something on the way home." He passed a series of plates around the table, ensuring everyone had enough. "Tully, Ellie, I know you're like, *totally watching your figures,* but I promise this stuff is all healthy."

Emilia smiled at Nick's playfulness as the kids all rolled their eyes. "Yes, eat up, please. Sal made the entire menu special for tonight."

"Yes," Cassio started, "and I can assure you that if you don't eat it, I will." He raised his brows, sending a warning sign to the twins, then winked at Luca. He'd only been on American soil for three hours, and he was already living up to his "fun uncle" reputation.

"You can't eat my food, Uncle Cass!" Luca giggled, shoveling a quick bite of fish in his mouth. "You—just—gotta—eat—yours."

"Luca, don't talk with your mouth full," Emilia warned before digging into her own plate, smiling all the same.

A new acoustic riff sounded in the background as Jacob began singing "Island in the Sun."

"Oh, I love this song," Luella said.

Tallulah immediately side-eyed her sister. "No, you don't."

Emilia rolled her eyes, knowing exactly where this was going.

"Yes, I do." Luella sat straighter in her seat, tossing her black hair over her shoulder, a trait she and her sister had acquired from their mother. "It's one of my favorites."

"What's it called?" Tallulah asked, taking a sip of her water.

"Shh," Luella said, waving her hand. "I love this part."

She began to sway, the doe-eyed expression on her face enough to give any lie away.

"He's too old for you, Ellie," Nick said, his voice sterner than usual.

Their daughter had always been infatuated with boys, much more than Tallulah ever had been. Emilia and Nick had been enduring conversations like this since Luella was five and she'd told them she was going to marry the lead singer from One Direction.

"Wait." Cassio held one hand up and wiped his face with the other. "You think that guy is cute? He looks like Bob Marley's pop-punk love child. Like he should be on an island smoking reefer somewhere."

Emilia refrained from telling him the young man did, in fact, smell like marijuana upon arrival, knowing that would only make his bad-boy image even more appealing to Luella.

Instead, she said, "What do you guys think about the food? Should we keep anything on the permanent menu?"

That easily did the trick, veering the conversation from her daughter's love life. They discussed the dishes at length, and by the end of it, they'd decided to keep the cheese board for the rest of the summer season to see how it performed.

"You know," Cassio said, finishing off the last of his wine, "if this stuff continues to sell well after tonight, we could bring it back next year, make it a summer staple."

Emilia nodded, swallowing her own drink as excitement crept into her bones. "I was thinking the same thing. And we could even try out different flavors for each season—create that sense of urgency that marketing people are always talking about."

Her brother nodded, and Emilia felt a swell of pride in her chest. Although she'd never gone to college, she'd always had a knack for this stuff, and since taking over Fiore Vineyards, it was like a faucet had been turned on, one she couldn't—and didn't want to—turn off. She found herself awake late at night, scrolling Pinterest and TikTok for inspiration on how to advance the business in the next quarter. Sunset vinyasas, wine barrel tastings, sommelier training classes; they all lived rent-free in her head.

"I even think," Cassio started but then held up a finger when his phone rang. Emilia watched his facial expression change.

"Sorry," he said, frowning at the screen. "I have to take this. Please excuse me."

"Yes, no worries." She made a shooing motion with her hand. "Go, go. We can talk later."

Cassio gave her a curt nod, then quickly walked off, leaving his chair out in the aisle.

"You'd think your brother would have better manners by now." Nick stood from his own seat, scooting it in before doing the same to Cassio's.

Emilia raised her hands in mock defeat. "Hey, don't look at me. I didn't raise him."

Nick continued to mumble under his breath as he gathered the empty plates from the table.

"Mom, can we please leave now?"

The question came from Luella, but Emilia knew she was speaking for both herself and her sister. Tallulah's lack of eye contact confirmed her suspicions.

"You can go see your friends," Emilia said. "But don't wander off the grounds. And keep your phones on!"

Luella and Tallulah weren't listening, though. They were already shuffling out of their seats, giggling about something Emilia would never be privy to.

Nick, noticing their lack of response, raised his voice as they scurried off. "We're serious, girls! Keep your ringers on, and be back here by eleven—not a second later."

"We will, Dad!" Tallulah threw her voice over her shoulder before blowing a quick kiss.

"Mommy, can I go play?"

Emilia turned to look at her five-year-old son. "I'm sorry, baby, but you're too little to go off on your own like your sisters." Luca started to object, so she quickly added, "How about you and I go light some sparklers together, and then you can have a piece of chocolate cake?"

His little face perked up at her words. "Oooo, okay! That sounds like fun. Let's go! Come on, Mommy! Bye, Daddy!"

Emilia and Nick laughed in unison as Luca tugged her toward the fields.

"Keep an eye on the girls for me, if you can?" Her voice came out like a question, knowing it would be totally uncool if they followed them, but also knowing times weren't like they used to be when she was a teen and could roam the grounds freely.

"Sure thing, babe." Nick blew her a kiss, then continued cleaning the table, and Emilia smiled as she watched her daughters run off in the distance.

If only she'd known that was the last night she'd ever see them.

EMILIA
NOW

SITTING BACK ON THE edge of the cliff after returning from her office, Emilia popped open one of the bottles of wine she'd snagged, not even bothering with a glass.

Below her, the waves continued to crash loudly against the rocks, the mist from the sea rising and coating the hair on her arms. The sight, sound, smell—all of the senses combined made her chest constrict as she realized this would be the last time she would experience this. The wondrous nature of the earth, its beauty on full display for the world to see.

She'd always wished she was that brave, that confident.

It doesn't matter. None of it matters without them.

The horrible thoughts slid into the crevices of her mind, and she shuddered, returning the bottle to her lips.

After several swigs, she pulled her gaze down to the label: *Lavanda Blanc.* The stupid wine had been a hit, but after what happened, she'd pulled it from the shelves immediately, not wanting the constant reminder of *that night*. Nick had begged her, pleaded with her, to let them sell it for the business's sake, but she'd refused. Nothing good could ever come from this wine, and if they sold it—well, it might as well be blood money.

She downed another long swig, willing the alcohol to do its job so she could do hers.

As if on cue, the papers she'd stuffed in her pocket poked out, caught in the wind. Emilia hated the idea of leaving Luca behind. He was her baby; he still needed a mother and was dealing with his own grief.

But she knew she couldn't be the mother he needed.

She didn't deserve him, or his love.

And quite frankly, he didn't deserve her either.

Because he deserved better. Luca was worthy of a parent who could be there for him in his time of need, not someone who was so absorbed in their own misery that they couldn't appreciate or take care of the beautiful child he was. Luca deserved a parent like Nick, and that was exactly what she was going to give him.

Only Nick.

Gritting her teeth, Emilia withdrew the crumpled papers and began to smooth them out. She'd never been much of a writer, but she had a brief idea of what she wanted to say. *It's not your fault. I love you. I'm sorry.* Something along those lines would convey how truly remorseful yet ill she was. Because she didn't want to cause her husband any more pain. She didn't even really want to kill herself. But the small voice inside her head said otherwise.

It had begun controlling and manipulating her several months ago when the police search started to wear out, yielding few results. She'd felt the thoughts, the tendencies, creeping in long before that, but hope was still alive in her chest. She still believed her children would come home to her one day, and that fuel ignited a fire deep within her, allowing her to block out the thoughts.

But then slowly, over time, her hope started to falter. With each dead end and useless lead, her skin resigned to dust, the ashes of her belief wavering until she couldn't take it anymore.

Emilia could no longer live with the grief, the guilt, the pain of losing Luella and Tallulah. And deep down, she hoped Luca would come to understand this in his own time. He would be angry at first, she knew that, but when he was old enough, she hoped Nick would give him the letter so he could finally have closure.

A seagull cawed in the distance, capturing her attention. Emilia watched the bird nosedive into the ocean, then flap to the shore with the rest of its flock. She continued watching for a few minutes, a numbness taking over her body as she disassociated from time and space. Maybe, just maybe, if she sat here long enough, she could imagine none of it ever happened. That things were back to the way they'd always been, and she'd never had to endure the awful atrocities that had trampled her life.

Your life is dead in the water. Better to join it below.

She clenched her jaw, squeezing her eyes shut as the thought ran through her.

"Okay," she choked out after a moment. "I'm going to do it. Just let me write this letter."

Emilia

Then

"Nick! Nick, wake up."

Emilia grabbed her husband's shoulders, drastically shaking him out of his slumber.

"Nick, please, *wake up*."

He mumbled something unintelligible, and Emilia gently smacked his face. That did the trick. "What?" he asked, his voice on the cusp of annoyed.

"The girls," Emilia said. "The girls never came home."

Finally understanding the urgency in her tone, Nick sat up and wiped the sleep from his eyes. "What do you mean? They were supposed to be with your brother."

Emilia shook her head. "That's what I'm saying. He never came home, either. I've been calling them, but no one will answer." She paused, staring at her husband in the illuminated darkness as the crest of twilight shone through the window. "I think something's wrong."

At this, Nick leaned over the bed and grabbed his phone, turning on a lamp in the process. It was nearing 5:00 a.m., and Cassio had promised to bring the girls straight home from the vineyard. The party had ended just after eleven, but Tallulah and Luella hadn't wanted to leave, claiming they wanted to hang out by the bonfire a little longer with their friends. Emilia had been hesitant, but then

Cassio offered to stay and bring them home later. Considering Emilia trusted her brother with her life, she'd said yes.

A decision she would forever regret.

"I'm sure it's fine." Nick held his phone to his ear, no doubt calling Tully, then Ellie. When he dialed Cassio and still didn't get a response, his expression faltered.

Emilia stood, the panic rising in her throat. "I told you—something's off."

"I admit it looks bad, but babe, it's also five in the morning. Wherever they are, I'm sure they're sleeping." He started redialing everyone as Emilia paced. Then, despite his previous statement, he stood, shuffling toward the closet where he retrieved his sneakers. "I'm sure they're fine. We just need to find them."

Emilia nodded, relieved her husband was taking this more seriously now. He thought they were okay, but the pit in her stomach told her otherwise. Something was wrong—she knew it.

"I'm coming with you," Emilia said, throwing open a drawer.

Nick shook his head. "No, someone has to stay here with Luca."

Emilia cursed under her breath, first with frustration, but then with mounting, aching dread.

Without another word, she bolted down the hallway, nearly busting Luca's door down in the process.

He's okay.

He's alive.

A wave of relief rushed through her at the sight of her sleeping son, but then another surge of adrenaline rippled in her chest as her thoughts landed back on the girls.

"Honey—" Nick started, but Emilia cut him off.

"He's okay," she said, tears running down her cheeks. "He's okay, my baby, he's okay." She swiped at the tears, shaking her head. "But my girls aren't. Please, go find them, Nick. Bring them home."

The fear that initially stabbed her now paralyzed her chest, radiating slowly throughout her entire body. Nick kissed her and assured her the twins were fine and he'd bring them home soon. She simply nodded, then crawled into bed with Luca, the tangible feeling of his small body next to hers the only ounce of comfort she would allow herself.

"WHAT DO YOU MEAN you didn't find them?"

Emilia stood in the doorway, having greeted her husband before he even made it inside.

"I went by the winery and Cassio's hotel. Nothing yet." He walked past her into the house, then pulled out his phone.

"Who are you calling now?"

His response was immediate. "The police."

They locked eyes as the words rolled off his tongue, and Emilia suddenly felt like she couldn't breathe. The idea that her children were missing was any parent's worst nightmare. The stuff you read about in the papers, see depicted in the movies. But never something you experience in your own life. You fear for it but mistakenly trust it'll never happen to your kids. That you're doing everything in your willpower to protect them, to ensure nothing bad ever happens to them, never once truly believing you could be wrong.

She clutched her chest, nearly falling to the floor as her lungs seized. This was never supposed to happen, not to her girls.

"Mommy, what's wrong?"

Luca's voice shocked Emilia's senses, but she couldn't speak, not yet. Instead, she looked for support from Nick, who quickly understood.

"Mommy's okay, sweetie," he said, scooping their child up in his arms. "There's just been a mix-up, and we're trying to find out where your sisters and Uncle Cass went last night."

Luca scrunched his little white brows together, a near-perfect image of his father. "Did they go back to Italy?"

Her son's question sent a chill down her spine.

"What do you mean, honey?" Emilia straightened, trying to understand.

"Last night, Luella said she wanted to go to Italy with Uncle Cass, and he said they could go sometime." He started to pick his nose, but Nick stopped him, pulling his hand down. "I told them I wanted to go too, but they said I was too little."

"Oh," Nick said, a small, sad smile playing on his lips. "I don't think they went to Italy, buddy. Your sisters don't even have a passport."

"A passport?" Luca asked, raising his voice. "What's a passport?"

Emilia's heart squeezed at the innocent question, and she held her hands out toward Luca, taking him so Nick could finish dialing the police. "Come on, sweetie, let's finish your pancakes while Daddy makes a couple phone calls."

Luca shrugged, then dodged his mom's grasp before skipping back into the kitchen and climbing onto his seat at the island. Though she was still terrified about her daughters' whereabouts, she sent a silent *thank you* to whatever deity would listen, grateful she could still protect her son's innocence.

Emilia spent the next hour calling everyone she knew, all while practically burning a hole in the rug from pacing so much. No one had seen the girls or Cass since the party last night. After the sixteenth call, which yielded similar results, Emilia clenched her fists together in anger. This wasn't supposed to be this hard. Surely, someone had seen them, or at least a trace of them. They were beautiful half-Italian teenage girls with long tan legs and dark hair down to their waists. They were also identical, and truthfully, they stood out in a crowd. Emilia had been certain someone would have spotted them by now, especially considering the tight-knit community they lived in. Cape Cod may be a tourist town, but they were like family with so many of the locals.

She bit the inside of her lip as another thought occurred to her. All of the regulars knew her daughters, and if none of them had seen them, then that meant a tourist might have—

No.

She couldn't think that.

Wasn't ready to face that possibility yet.

A loud knock sounded at the door, pulling her from her thoughts. She moved at lightning speed, knowing time was of the essence. She'd watched enough true crime documentaries to know that with each passing breath, they were less likely to find her daughters. They only had seventy-two hours before the police switched their terminology from *bringing them home alive* to *finding their bodies.*

"Hello, officers," she said, swinging the door open. "Thank you for coming."

She was shocked, yet thankful, to see not one but two officers standing on her porch. One was a tall strawberry-blond man with fair skin, and the other was a short dark-skinned woman with black hair tucked into a low bun.

"Hello, ma'am. I'm Officer John Holt, and this is Officer Kiersten Winding," the male cop said pointing to the female. "We received a call about a missing person?"

"Persons," Emilia corrected automatically. "Missing persons. My brother was supposed to bring my teenage twin daughters home last night, but we haven't seen or heard from any of them all morning."

Officer Holt pulled out a notepad, then gestured to the door. "May we come inside?"

"Yes, yes, of course." Emilia nodded, stepping aside so the two could come in. Once they'd both entered, she closed the door and yelled for Nick.

A moment later, he came running down the stairs with Luca in his arms. His eyes widened as he registered the cops' presence. "Hello, officers. Just a moment; let me set him down in there."

"Why are there cops here? Are you and Mommy bad guys?" Luca blurted out as Nick rushed him off to the living room before dumping him with a snack and headphones.

"Sorry about that," Nick said, gliding back into the foyer a moment later. "He learned about cops in school and has been a bit obsessed."

Officer Winding smiled, shaking Nick's hand. "My son's the same way."

"Oh, how old is he?" Nick asked, pleasant as always despite the severity of the situation.

"Just turned four," she said, still smiling.

"So, you said your daughters are missing?" Officer Holt asked, clearing his throat.

Emilia, thankful for his sense of urgency, said, "Yes. Tallulah and Luella. My brother was supposed to bring them home last night, but he didn't. We haven't been able to reach any of them all morning, and this just isn't like them."

"Is it possible they're staying at his place?"

"No," Emilia said. "Cassio lives in Italy. He only came here for a business trip. We own the local winery, Fiore Vineyards. My brother is a partner, and he was in town for the festival we held last night."

Holt continued to scribble a few notes.

"And you've tried calling them?" Winding asked.

Emilia stared at her blankly, trying to hide her burning anger. "Yes, of course we did. I already said that. We've called and texted a million times with no response. I'm telling you, something is wrong."

"Apologies, ma'am, we just have to ask all the obvious questions so nothing goes amiss," Holt said as he held up a hand. "Now tell us, what time did you last see them?"

Emilia quickly recounted the previous night's events, frustration and hope and anxiety all swelling in her chest.

"Is there anywhere else your brother may have taken them? Perhaps to another family member's house or a boyfriend's place?" Winding's question was like a punch to the gut.

"No," Nick said, cutting in. "We don't have any other family here, and Cassio may not have kids of his own, but he knows better than to take our teenage girls to a boy's house without our permission." He shook his head, dismissing the thought. "No. We don't know where they are. I went by the business this morning, then to his hotel. Didn't see any signs of them."

"Wait," Holt said, looking up from his notes. "You said you went to the vineyard and his hotel this morning?"

"Yes," Nick said, rolling his lips in and nodding fervently. "I thought maybe the girls had some wine after we left and that Cass might be letting them sleep it off so they wouldn't get in trouble with us, but nothing seemed amiss at work. And nobody answered the door at the hotel. I tried asking for a key, explaining the situation to the person at the front desk, but they wouldn't give me one."

Holt wrote furiously without missing a beat. "And what time was that?"

Nick blew out a breath, then rubbed the back of his neck. "I don't know. You woke me up at what, five, babe?" He looked at Emilia for confirmation, continuing when she nodded. "I left here right after, so I must've been at the vineyard around 5:15, 5:20. I went to the hotel right after."

Too much time was passing. Emilia couldn't stand it. If they didn't start looking soon, then they'd risk—

"And where were you two last night?"

Emilia blinked, looking at Winding, who'd asked the question. "We each went home after the party ended, around eleven or a little after."

"And you were home all night?" she persisted.

"Yes," Emilia said, frustration feathering her bones. "Nick put Luca to bed, and I crashed as soon as I got in."

She was hoping that would be the end of that line of questioning when Officer Holt asked, "Is there anyone else who can corroborate your story? Besides the two of you."

Nick's face looked stung. "You mean like an alibi?"

Holt gave him a tight nod in response.

"Officer, if you're insinuating we had something to do with this—"

Winding cut Nick off. "We're not insinuating anything. We simply have to follow protocol, cross our t's and dot our i's, so to speak. In cases like this, the parents are always the first suspects. We're just doing our part to help clear your names so we can focus on finding your family."

Nick looked like he was going to get angry, so Emilia grabbed his hand, letting her gentle touch soothe his nerves. "It's okay; we understand. Thank you for doing everything you can. We just want to know our daughters are safe."

"And your brother," Winding added.

"What?" Emilia cocked her head.

"You said you want to know your daughters are safe," she repeated. "But your brother is missing, too."

"Oh," Emilia said, letting out a breath and nodding. "Yes, yes, of course, I hope he's safe, too, but as a mother, I'm sure you can understand why my fears are mostly geared toward my girls."

Officer Winding stared at her for a moment, and Emilia felt the scrutiny as she studied her, considering her words. Anger continued to lap at Emilia's chest, but she took slow, anchoring breaths, not wanting to crack under the pressure. Yes, she cared about her brother, but her brother was a grown-ass man who, quite frankly, was responsible for her children's well-being last night. The fact that he didn't bring them home to her had her all the more angry.

But she couldn't show this, couldn't admit this to the cops. Winding was looking for every reason to accuse them of something, and while it pissed Emilia off to no end, she knew she had to play nice if she wanted them to leave her alone and look for her children. Thankfully, she had a lot of practice. As a woman, she'd had to mask her emotions like this her entire life.

Apparently, being a woman didn't change a damn thing for Officer Winding.

"We hope they are *all* safe," Nick said, cutting in and dismantling the tension in the room. "Please. We just want you to find our family. This isn't normal behavior for any of them."

Emilia thanked her lucky stars that her husband hadn't added *even Luella* to his statement.

Finally, the two officers nodded and thanked them for their time.

"I promise," Holt said on his way out, "we will do everything in our power to find your daughters and brother."

Nick and Emilia both mumbled a thanks, just as Winding's phone rang.

"Please excuse me," she said, holding up a finger and turning around. "Officer Winding."

Emilia, Nick, and Officer Holt exchanged polite, albeit awkward, glances at each other as Winding mumbled a few "uh-huhs" and "hmms" on the phone. After a few minutes of strained silence, she thanked the other person on the line and hung up.

Then, slowly, she turned back around, facing Nick. "You said you went to Fiore Vineyards this morning, around 5:20?"

Although confused, Nick nodded. "Yes. Yes, that's right."

"And where did you look?"

Emilia turned her gaze to Nick now, panic stirring in her veins.

"I walked across the entire grounds, then checked the buildings."

Winding's expression deadpanned. "You went inside the office building?"

"Yes," he said, standing a little straighter. "What's this about?"

Instead of responding to Nick, she turned her attention to Holt. "That was the chief. He said someone just reported a dead body. A male found in the office hall closet at Fiore Vineyards."

Emilia
Now

EMILIA LAY ON THE rocky terrain, staring at the sky.

After trying, and failing, to write her letter for over an hour, she'd given up, succumbing to the stormy sea inside her head. She had so much she wanted to say, but every time she tried, thoughts of *that night* interjected, a syringe of grief and betrayal bleeding into her skull.

Failure.

She closed her eyes, the sunny presence in the sky no match for the darkness that lingered in her mind.

"You can do this," she whispered to herself. "You *have* to do this."

Except you don't, the voice inside her said. *We could just roll off this cliff together, right now, and you'll never have to—*

"Enough!" she screamed, cutting the voice off as the numbness in her chest tingled, frustration taking over. "Just stop." She slid her hands onto her face, then dug her nails into the soft flesh of her skin, willing the physical pain to silence the intrusion in her brain. "Just, make it . . . stop."

A stinging sensation prickled in the middle of her forehead, and she let out a gasp, releasing her grip. Then, after a few more laboring breaths, she sat up slowly, mere inches from the cliff's one-hundred-foot drop. Emilia chanced a peek over the ledge, inhaling the ocean's runaway mist as memories of her mamma surfaced. This was where they'd taken their secret picnics when Emilia was a young girl. Her mother made her promise not to go too close to the edge, drawing a line in the sand with her toe.

"You're not to go past this line, Emmy," she'd said. "*Pericoloso.*"

Dangerous.

Emilia smirked at the word now, remembering how freeing it'd felt to scatter her mamma's and papà's ashes over this same cliff. The ashes of their hearts would forever remain woven into the sea, lapping against the beach's shoreline, rising in the ocean's mist, coating the vineyard's landscape in quiet dewdrops, infiltrating the nose, then the lungs of everyone there.

It was a beautiful concept.

Emilia's phone rang, making her jump. Sighing, she pulled the device from her pocket, blinking rapidly as her eyes adjusted to the tiny screen.

Husband Calling.

Emilia groaned. She did not want to talk to Nick right now. At least not really. Sure, she was attempting to write him a letter, but that's because speaking to him directly would be too hard. Hearing his voice would shatter her.

So, instead of accepting the call, she declined it, turned the ringer off, and returned her attention to the sea.

You can't forget him that easily.

She whimpered at the malicious voice in her head.

Because of course she couldn't forget Nick. Her sweet, sweet husband, who'd once been the sun she revolved around. He would be so upset with her once he discovered what she did, but at some level, she hoped he'd come to understand. Because losing the twins had hurt him, too, changed him in ways that had broken Emilia's heart. He used to be so radiant, so full of joy and hope, but that ended the moment they got the call about Cassio's body. Nick became an instant suspect then, and that, combined with the dreaded loss of their girls, had nearly broken him.

He told the police he hadn't thought to check the small storage closet where Zoey had found Cassio's body, claiming he didn't think it big enough to house a dead body. He'd simply walked inside the office, done a quick walk-through of all the rooms, and left when he hadn't seen anything unordinary. The cops corroborated his story quickly enough, but the accusation alone had left a mark on him.

Then, one by one, as the days and weeks went on, she watched as another one of his rays dampened, the light in his eyes slowly extinguishing into a haze. She'd always believed he'd been the one to affect her, always brightening up her darkened view of life, but now the roles were reversed. She was still the moon, and he was still the sun, but now she overpowered him, rolled into his line of vision, and turned their life into a solar eclipse.

She hated herself for it.

Her phone vibrated again in her pocket, and her heart squeezed. Before even looking at the screen, she knew it was her husband again. How would she ever go through with this if he kept interrupting her?

Confirming it was, in fact, Nick calling again, she sent him to voicemail, then turned off the phone. She couldn't bear to hear his voice right now.

It would hurt too much.

It would all hurt too much.

It'll hurt less soon, the intrusive, domineering voice whispered in her head. *You'll finally be freed of the pain, the guilt, when you get where you're going.*

"But *where* am I going?" Emilia whispered back.

Because that was the question that still plagued her, still haunted her dreams, still made her living nightmare that much more unbearable.

Because if there really was a God, the one and only ruler of the universe who supposedly sent his only son to die on the cross for her sins, then why hadn't he brought her girls home? Why had he allowed any of this to happen? Why did she still feel this useless, endless void of pain and sorrow?

Don't worry about that, the voice said, making Emilia feel violated by her entire soul being on display. *It'll all be better soon.*

Not knowing what else to do, she picked up her bottle of wine, chugging the rest of it before tossing it over the ledge and opening a second one.

"Okay," she whispered in a shaky breath. "Okay."

With trembling hands, she picked up the pencil and paper and tried again.

Emilia

Then

THE VINEYARD WAS DRAPED in black, her magical oasis transformed into a sea of despair.

Emilia sat in the front row, staring at the urn that now held her brother's ashes. They'd closed the business for the weekend, long enough to hold Cassio's funeral, the same way they'd done with her mamma and papà. The entire family was supposed to be laid to rest here; it was something they'd agreed to a long time ago. Emilia just never thought she'd have to witness another funeral and the ceremonial scattering of ashes over the edge of the cliff so soon.

She prayed this would be the only funeral she attended this year, that the police would find her daughters alive and bring them home to her sooner rather than later. When they'd initially received the news about Cassio's body, Emilia felt relieved and terrified at the same time. Because while she was thankful her daughters weren't also found dead, that meant they were still out there. Still at the hands of the monster who had done this to her brother.

She couldn't stand the thought.

Nick cleared his throat beside her, giving her a small nudge. Emilia pulled herself from her thoughts and turned toward the priest, who, up until this point, had been spewing words of sentimental value Emilia didn't care to comprehend.

But now, his eyes were centered on her, insinuating it was time for the eulogy. The eulogy that, if she were being honest, she hadn't even wanted to write, let alone stand in front of a crowd and perform. Because even though Cassio was dead, she still blamed him for what happened to Tallulah and Luella. He was the grown-up, their *uncle*. He was supposed to be keeping them safe. She'd trusted him with their lives, and he hadn't even been man enough to keep his own life intact.

What a horrible mistake she'd made.

"Babe?" Nick whispered. "Are you okay? Do you need me to read it for you?"

Emilia shook her head, stifling the tears that threatened her mascara. "I'm okay. I can do it."

Slowly, she stood, smoothing her dress as her hands shook. The priest smiled at her, and she did her best imitation of a smile back at him, obviously fooling no one.

Once she felt steady enough to walk, she trudged through the grass, careful not to let her heels sink into the ground. Then, as she closed the distance between herself and the podium, she finally turned to face the crowd before her.

Several of their relatives had flown in from Italy and were seated in the first few rows. She scanned their faces, making eye contact with each of them as she tried to find the strength to do this. Then, with a wink from her aunt, *Zia* Giana, Emilia swallowed. *"Grazie per essere qui oggi. Se per tutti va bene, vorrei continuare in inglese."*

She looked back to her family members, awaiting their approval to continue in English. Seeing several nods, Emilia took a deep breath and started again. "Hello, thank you all for being here today." She paused, feeling a lump in her throat.

You have to do this.

But did she? Did she really have to deliver a eulogy when two pieces of her heart were out there, somewhere in the world, doing God knows what with God knows who? It wasn't fair.

None of it was fair.

Play the part. Just get it over with.

Sighing, she brushed away a stray tear and tried again. "Cassio may have been a partial business owner here, but he was also many other things. A son, a brother, an—"

Uncle.

Her voice broke before she could even say the word.

Because he didn't deserve the title.

Hadn't earned it.

An involuntary pain squeezed her chest, then her sides, and before she knew it, the rest of her words were stuck, strangled in the sea of spit that gurgled in her throat. Her gaze diverted from the eulogy's pages to the audience in front of her, then to Nick, her sweet anchor who seemed to understand everything from that one glimpse alone.

Without a sound, he rose from his seat and swiftly came to her side, retrieving the papers with one hand and holding hers with the other.

EMILIA FELT LIKE BREAKING the glass in her hand.

After scattering Cassio's ashes into the sea, she'd been more than ready to go home, but their guests had other ideas. Between the local townspeople and her visiting relatives, everyone had collectively agreed to stay and drink wine, in honor of Cass's memory. Emilia was still nursing her first glass, too nauseous for camaraderie and cheer.

Thankfully, she didn't have to play nice anymore. Because just as she was on the brink of squeezing her glass too tight, the phantom feeling of shards breaking against her skin, she spotted two cops making their way across Fiore's grounds.

"So sorry, pardon me," she said unapologetically as she pushed past her *Zia* Giana and shoved the wineglass into her hand.

A flutter of hope beat in her chest as she ran toward the officers, the way it always did any time she spoke with them. *Did you find them? Are there any leads?* These were the questions that plagued her heart, often falsifying hope.

Today, she dreamed her hopes would be real.

"Officers," she said, nearly out of breath. "How can I help you? Have you found something?"

Officer Holt spoke first. "Afternoon, ma'am. Condolences on your brother."

Emilia stared at the man, all six feet whatever of him, and could almost puke from his politeness in the situation.

Officer Winding wasn't as sentimental. "We'd like to talk to you for a few minutes, if you can find the time in all your . . . grief."

The way she said it was like a slap to the face. Despite ruling out Emilia and Nick's possible involvement in this case, Winding had continued treating both of them like suspects.

Emilia did her best to cooperate, though, because these were the only people who could help find her girls. "Yes, of course." She smoothed an untamed hair out of her face, attempting to slick it back into the low bun she was sporting.

"At this point in time, we have no other leads on the whereabouts of your daughters." Holt's words hit the air, reverberating off Emilia's eardrums and landing in the hollow pit of her chest. "But," he continued, "we were wondering . . . have you seen anyone unusual here today?"

Emilia cocked her head to the side, rubbing the back of her neck. "I . . . I don't know." She'd been on the brink of a panic attack so many times today. Survival had been her only focus, not identifying the myriad of faces that surrounded her.

Winding shifted her stance, crossing her arms across her chest and taking on the outdated role of bad cop. "The perpetrator will oftentimes return to the scene of a crime or the funeral of their victim."

"What, why?" Emilia did a double take over her shoulder before returning her attention to Winding.

"Various reasons," Winding continued. "To get a thrill from reliving the crime—"

"Or to show remorse in an attempt to atone for their sins," Holt said, cutting in.

Emilia rubbed the bridge of her nose, staving off a tension headache. "So you're saying whoever did this to Cass, and whoever has the girls . . ."

"They could be here today, yes." Winding's voice was softer this time, and for once, Emilia was grateful. The idea that the person who took her sweet Tallulah and Luella could be here, just lurking in the background, getting off on it while her insides crumbled, was enough to make her faint.

"So," Winding continued, "have you seen anyone unusual here today?"

Emilia wanted to answer yes, to find the exact person to lay blame on and watch their world blow up in shambles the way hers had, but the truth was, she hadn't noticed anyone of significant interest. She'd been too caught up in her own grief, her own trauma, to be the mother her children needed her to be.

The weight of the realization was suffocating.

"I wasn't paying attention before, but let me take another look around," she pleaded.

The officers exchanged a glance, their attempted subtlety not going unnoticed.

"What?" Emilia asked, her heart palpitating. "What are you not saying?"

Her eyes bounced back and forth between the two, willing them to speak. A gust of wind rolled by, punctuating their silence. Her skin prickled.

Finally, Holt spoke. "We are doing everything we can to locate your daughters, but as you know, at this time, we have no suspects."

Emilia nodded, biting her bottom lip. They'd told her this a million times. "Yes, I know, which is why you're working to find suspects, right? Why you're here today."

Another cautious glance passed between the two police officers.

"Emilia," Winding said, "what we're saying is, if we can't produce a lead soon, this case may dry up."

Something like anger burned just beneath Emilia's skin. "What?" she said. "You mean like a cold case?" Seeing both the officers nodding, she felt the swell of fury inside her rising to the surface. "They've only been missing for two weeks. How could this possibly be a cold case?"

"We're not saying that yet," Holt said, raising a hand. "We just wanted you to be aware that without any leads, there's only so much we can do."

Emilia shook her head. "No, absolutely not." She looked each of them square in the face. "That is an unacceptable answer. You two have a job to do. You have to keep working, trying to find them." Her voice was rising now, but she didn't care.

Winding's stern tone overpowered Emilia's. "Miss, we are doing our due diligence, but so far, no one has come forward with new evidence, there have been no sightings of the girls, and the last person to see them alive is now dead."

This wasn't making sense. They'd barely started looking. Emilia refused to believe this was the end of the line.

"So try a new tactic!" she screamed. "Investigate Cassio. Who was he involved with? I mean, there's got to be a reason my brother ended up dead the same night my children went missing."

Her chest heaved as she stared at the two of them, incredulous.

"Are you saying your brother was involved in shady dealings?"

Winding's question made her want to laugh.

Instead, she flexed her jaw. "I don't know what I'm saying other than the fact that you two need to try harder. If all you're doing is asking me for the information, it's pretty obvious you're not doing enough yourselves." She muttered something in Italian under her breath. "Where is that detective you introduced me to? Why is he not here?"

"As we've said, miss," Winding started, "we have no suspects at this point. If that changes, you'll be hearing from Detective Rollings."

"*If?*" Emilia's jaw dropped. "What do you mean, 'if'?" Then without giving them a chance to answer, she erupted in anger. "Is this what our country's legal system has come to? Children go missing, and you all, the *one group* of people who are supposed to be dedicated to keeping them safe, to bringing them home, just throw in the towel if *we* don't provide *you* with a suspect?"

"Mrs. Davenport—" Officer Holt tried to cut in, but Emilia wasn't having it.

"No, this is bullshit," she spat. "You two need to do your jobs, and for the love of God"—she spun around, pointing her finger toward Winding—"stop treating me and my husband like we had something to do with this. It's insulting, quite frankly. We just want our kids to come home."

Her voice broke into a sob as familiar arms encircled her waist.

"Officers," Nick said, his steady presence a stark contrast to hers.

Winding and Holt rambled on in the background, but Emilia wasn't listening to them anymore. She wasn't listening to anyone. Her emotional walls were falling down, and suddenly, she couldn't take it.

"Nick," she said through an exaggerated breath.

He squeezed her in response and then dismissed the cops. "It's okay, baby," he said. "I'm here."

EMILIA
NOW

THE FUCKING COPS.

Emilia finished writing, her disappointment in the legal system just as palpable now as it was a year ago. How is it that a person in uniform could hold so much power yet squander it all away? Emilia had seen dozens of true crime films, watched all the popular shows regarding missing persons cases, but she'd never understood the characters' immense need to *start up a search party* or *take matters into their own hands.*

That is, until she lived it. After Holt and Winding had mentioned the case potentially going cold during Cassio's funeral, it was only a matter of time before their threat became real. Leads dried up, new kids went missing, and suddenly, no one was concerned with finding her girls anymore.

So she'd taken matters into her own hands.

She'd held search parties, scoured the internet for clues. Hell, she'd even started attending church again, asking for prayers and suffering through the pitying looks of strangers. Emilia had done everything to find her children.

Everything.

But it wasn't enough.

It was never enough.

She had failed her twins, time and time again, and the guilt all but consumed her.

A wave broke on the rocky shoreline beneath her just then, and Emilia wondered what it would feel like when her body did the same.

It's time.

She clutched the papers in her hand, obeying the voice in her head. Her letter was finished, and with its completion came a sudden sense of finality. This was it. This was all her life would ever be, all her parents' legacy would ever become: a fractured skull and missing heart, still somewhere out there bleeding for her girls.

I'm so sorry, Mamma and Papà, her heart whispered. She closed her eyes against the cool, gentle breeze.

Ti amo.

Soon, she would join them in the sea, departing from the same cliff. The only difference being that her body was firm, solid.

That would change soon enough, though.

While she didn't know what would happen to her in the afterlife, or even if there was an afterlife, she'd read about the decomposition process thoroughly. First, if she were lucky, her body would die on impact. Then, immediately after, the decomposition process would begin, the water accelerating its rate. Her body would go through a series of chemical changes as she passed from fresh, to active, to advanced decay, withering away until all that was left were skeletal remains.

In a way, she would still be ashes in the sea, just like the rest of her family. Knowing this brought her an odd sense of comfort.

Her only wish was that if her daughters were ever found, Nick would bring them to the sea to visit her.

She brushed a tear away from her sunken cheek, then stood, dusting her hands off on her ivory dress. The weight of the letter clung to her like an anchor, holding her down until she felt an overwhelming, drowning sensation *to tear it, rip it apart. Never leave it.*

The intrusive thoughts suffocated her. This letter contained her last dying wishes, her one attempt to help Nick raise their baby boy without her, to let him know how sorry she was, and to explain just how much she loved them. She had to leave these papers for him.

Feeling the frantic panic building in her chest, Emilia searched the ground for a rock large enough to hold the papers in place. She could walk back across the vineyard to leave the letter in the office, but that would take too long, and time was of the essence.

Emilia.

"No," she whispered. *No, no, no.* She wouldn't let the voice win out; she couldn't.

To her left, she spotted a rock sticking out of the ground that looked large enough to hold the papers in place, yet not so heavy that she couldn't pull it out.

Stop.

The war within her head continued to rage, and she fell to her knees, clawing at the dirt in a desperate attempt to free the small boulder. If she could just break it free—

Enough! the sinister voice commanded yet again. *No one will care why you're gone. They're better off without you, and you know it. Your family deserves better than anything you could give them.*

She fell backward, crumpling the papers in the process, and began to sob.

Because he was right.

The voice inside her head was always right.

And so, even though it was the last thing she wanted, the last possible option she could've chosen, Emilia obeyed the devil inside her. She pulled out her cell phone long enough to turn it on and send Nick a quick text: *Goodbye. I love you, and I'm sorry. Please hug Luca for me.* And then she chucked it over the cliff, along with the letter.

NICK
NOW

"Daddy, can we have a snack when we're all done with our sight words?"

Nick sat on the edge of his stool, staring into the gentle face of his kindergartener. "Sure, buddy." He ruffled Luca's wavy golden hair that resembled his own. "Whatever you want."

Luca cheered, and the smile that lit up on his face was enough to warm Nick's heart, if only for a moment. It had been nearly a year since Tallulah and Luella had gone missing from the winery. Three hundred and thirty-four days since he'd spoken to his daughters, seen their beautiful faces, heard their precious voices. It'd been eleven months since a part of his soul had burnt out, and Nick was starting to wonder if he'd ever find the light again.

"W-water," Luca said as he sounded out the letters. "That spells water!"

Nick smiled and nodded. "Good job, son. Just a few more."

He scooted the colorful sheets toward Luca, attempting to see the good in his everyday life, to be the best parent he could be for his little boy. At first, when the girls went missing, Nick was reluctant to admit he'd ignored his son, been too consumed with his own grief to be the father Luca needed. Nick would find him holed up in his room, lying under a blanket and crying. Other times, he'd find Luca drawing on the wall or intentionally making some other large mess, doing things that he was well beyond the age of knowing better not to do. When

Nick and Emilia brought this behavior up to the therapist, she'd said Luca was likely crying out for attention. Because as much as he may miss his sisters, he likely missed his parents more.

That was the moment everything shifted for Nick.

"You want Goldfish or animal crackers today?"

Luca finished sounding out another word from his sheet—*bubble*—before blurting, "Goldfish, please! And apple juice."

Nick moved across the expanse of their massive white kitchen, grazing the marble countertops as he went. It'd been five years since they had them installed. Nick and Emilia had both busted ass that summer, working endlessly to afford the upgrades they so desired to create the perfect home. If only they'd known how wasted their efforts would be.

Reaching the cupboard, Nick began pulling out the necessities for snack time: a bowl, the snack, the extra snack Luca always asked for, a cup, ice, juice. It was a mundane task at best, but one Nick was glad to have.

"Here you go—"

He'd started to turn around, but his phone rang, cutting him off. He used to keep it on silent, but ever since the girls went missing, he'd kept it fully charged with the ringer on high at all times, *just in case*.

Jamming his hand in his pocket, he pulled the device out, and his eyes grew wide at the familiar name on the screen.

"Holt," he said, nearly tripping over his feet. "How can I help you? Have there been any new leads?"

The next words that came out of the officer's mouth would forever be cemented in Nick's brain, marking it as the best day of his life.

"We found them, Nick."

Nick
Now

"Here," Nick said to his mother, Alice, shoving Luca's overnight bag into her arms as she opened the front door.

Alice nearly dropped the forkful of Tater Tot casserole she'd been nibbling on. "What is this? Nick, honey, you know I love Luca, but we're right in the middle of dinner for my book club, and some of this stuff gets a little *raunchy*, if you know what I mean."

But Nick wasn't listening. His thoughts were running a million miles a minute, the overwhelming need to see the girls again his only focus. He ushered Luca inside the foyer, and when it was clear Nick wasn't taking no for an answer, Alice started to protest again.

"Mom," he said loudly, interrupting her. She jumped at the sound of his voice, so he paused, cleared his throat, and tried again, covering Luca's ears. "They found them."

The weight of the words lifted from his chest, reverberating loudly in the space between them. Alice's eyes grew wide, and for a moment, neither of them spoke.

"Dad, I want a cookie!" Luca swatted his father's hands away, breaking the tension.

Alice waited for Luca to disappear into the house before she spoke. "Are they . . ." Her voice trailed, unable to complete the question.

Nick nodded, a sloppy grin forming on his face as his heart fluttered. "They're alive."

At that, Alice let out a sob and grabbed her son, pulling him into a full-on body hug. "Oh, thank God, son! Oh, praise Jesus. God is *so* good."

"All the time," Nick whispered back through his own tears. He pulled away from his mother, then wiped his eyes with the backs of his hands.

"So where are they? Are they okay? Do you know what happened?"

Nick bit his lip, shaking his head. "I don't know much yet. Cop just said to meet him at the hospital. Can you just take care of Luca for me, please? And don't tell him what's going on. I haven't explained anything yet."

Alice nodded. "Yes, yes, of course." She paused, placing a gentle hand against her son's cheek. "I'm just so happy they found them."

Nick shut his eyes, staving off more tears. "Me too."

He hugged his mom goodbye, then hightailed it back to his car. Once inside, he revved the engine and sped off, then called Emilia yet again. He'd been calling her nonstop since he hung up with Officer Holt, but the fact that she wasn't answering would've been more alarming if he weren't chasing the high of finally seeing Tully and Ellie. To know they were alive, safe and waiting for him, was absolutely everything.

After dialing her number again, and this time being sent straight to voicemail, Nick cursed, throwing his phone to the side. What could she possibly be doing that would cause her to ignore him, let alone not pick up? Nearly running through a red light, Nick swerved into the other lane as he continued to weave through traffic, then picked up his phone again at a stoplight.

Nick: *Call me back ASAP*

He clicked the phone shut yet again, but this time, he kept it gripped to his chest. The officer had said the girls were at West General Hospital, which was on the other side of town. Nick pressed his foot to the gas pedal once again, the adrenaline nearly suffocating him.

He had to see them. Had to know they were all right.

Had to know what had happened to them.

Holt hadn't told him any of the details on the phone, only that both girls were alive and brought to the hospital immediately after rescue. Nick had no idea what the hell that meant, but he would incur ten million speeding tickets if it meant he could find out one millisecond sooner.

His phone buzzed as he continued to zip through town, and he answered without looking. "Emmy?"

"No, honey, this is your mother."

Nick let out an exasperated breath. "What's wrong?"

"Nothing, nothing," Alice said, the distant sound of chaos ringing in the background of her receiver. "I just wanted to make sure it was okay with you if I took Luca to the park later."

Irritation seeped through Nick's pores. He appreciated his mom checking in, but he needed to keep the line clear for Emilia or Holt. "Yes, yes, that's fine. I don't care, as long as he's safe."

Alice scoffed. "Well, of course he's safe with me, Nick. I just know how overprotective Emilia can be. I tried calling her, but she didn't answer."

The way she said it only made Nick's frustration grow. "Just don't take your eyes off him, okay?" He blew out a breath, then cut off a semi, which respectfully earned him a honk and an honorary middle finger. "I love you, Mom, but I gotta go."

He hung up before she could finish speaking, then thumbed out another quick text to Emilia.

Nick: *Emmy, they found them. Call me.*

Another vehicle honked at Nick, and he slammed on his brakes, narrowly missing a head-on collision. He sat there for a moment, allowing his heart rate to stutter, and then he threw his phone down and gunned it yet again, closing the rest of the distance between him and his daughters.

BREATHE, HE TOLD HIMSELF.

Nick stepped off the elevator, putting one foot in front of the other so fast he nearly tripped multiple times. When he finally reached the nurses' station, a sheen of sweat glistened on his forehead.

"My daughters," he blurted before anyone had the chance to greet him. "My daughters, Tallulah and Luella Davenport. The police said they were here on this floor."

A woman with sun-kissed skin and freckles looked at him now, a mixed bag of emotions playing over her face. "Yes, sir, of course. They're in room—"

A hand clapped on his shoulder, and he jumped as Officer Holt spoke. "Nick."

Eyes wild, Nick turned and stared at the man. "Where are they?"

Holt waved at the nurse, then turned Nick toward the appropriate wing before descending down the long corridor. "They're just in there, room 200."

Anxiety and relief bubbled in his chest, and Nick tried to run in, but the police officer held him back.

"Nick," he said, his tone serious. "Before you go in there, you should know, they may not be receptive to you right away, and it may be difficult to see them in this condition. Your daughters have been through immense trauma."

Nick swallowed, searching the man's face for words left unsaid. Tears were brimming at the corners of Nick's eyes, and he wanted nothing more than to hold his little girls.

"What happened to them?" he asked before adding the deep-seated question, "Who took them?"

The officer held his gaze, a hint of sorrow reflecting in his golden irises. Then, after a monumental beat of silence, he cleared his throat and began. "We rescued your daughters from a sex trafficking ring."

NICK

NOW

"SEX TRAFFICKING?" NICK GAVE the man an incredulous look. "What do you mean?"

Officer Holt cast his gaze down as a nurse walked by, then looked back at Nick. "Our special forces unit has been working with the FBI to bring down a local sex trafficking ring. We've been investigating the matter for quite some time."

Panic stirred inside Nick. "But . . . but that kind of stuff doesn't happen here. This is a family-friendly area."

"Quite the contrary," Holt said, adjusting his stance. "Cape Cod is isolated from the mainland and a popular tourist location, making it an ideal spot for traffickers to source their victims. It's easier for them to quickly sell and move the children without getting caught. We are incredibly lucky to have found your children at all. Most cases like this?" He paused, shaking his head. "The victims are never found, much less so close to their home."

Nick's legs gave out beneath him as his world shifted.

"Hey, hey, easy there." Holt caught him and helped him into a nearby seat.

Tears pricked at the back of Nick's eyes, and he let his head fall into his hands. How the hell had this happened? He was so, so grateful to have his children back, to see them and take care of them again, but knowing the reality of where they'd been? Nick didn't know if he could handle that. The mere thought of someone touching his little girls made his body rage.

"Excuse me, miss, could he get some water?" Holt flagged down an aide, then patted Nick's face. "Hey, breathe, Dad. They're okay. We got them back."

Nick looked up at him, nodding. Then, he asked, "How did you find them? Were they—"

His voice hitched, unable to finish the question.

Holt continued to hold his gaze, his eyes steady yet gracious. "Our informant discovered the location where an expected trafficking attempt was set to take place, and our team was able to invade it, raiding the home and rescuing twenty-six children. Tallulah and Luella were among them. I recognized them right away."

A whimper escaped Nick's lips as he continued to cry, both for the joy that was to come and the sorrow he was discovering. As a father, it was his job to protect his children, and he'd failed—massively. He didn't know how he'd ever live with the guilt.

Finally, after taking a minute to gather himself, he asked, "Can I see them now? Please?"

Holt nodded, offering Nick a hand to help him stand. Slowly, the two walked toward the door, and Nick felt all his pent-up emotions begging to be released. Grief, hope, sorrow, guilt, joy, agony, relief. They all rattled inside his chest like caged birds doing anything but singing.

He placed his hand on the doorknob, but it trembled under his touch, giving him pause.

"Are you ready?" The officer's voice came from behind him now.

Nick swallowed, then nodded, carefully pushing the door open until he could see two beautiful sets of brown eyes staring back at him.

"Dad?"

EMILIA
NOW

FEELING LIBERATED FROM HER phone and, with it, her last connection to the real world, Emilia stood and began to undress.

She'd worn an old ivory-colored cotton gown her mother had sewn for her right after she'd given birth to Tully and Ellie. Emilia had been struggling with postpartum depression, and her mother had made the dress in an attempt to make her feel better. There was no size attached, only a simple "Made with Love" label her mamma had stitched in place for her. The dress hugged her in all the right places and was long and flowy without being overwhelmingly frumpy. It had been the sole representation of the birth of her new life. It only seemed fitting that Emilia wore it today.

Besides, wearing black felt too much like death.

Emilia wanted to feel like she was passing from one life to another, not dying from one life to no other.

Now, though, as Emilia stood on the cusp of the cliff from where the other members of her family had also departed, she felt a sensational urge to leave the dress behind. To fold it and leave it for whomever to find.

It didn't deserve to be ruined.

Carefully, she slid the inch-wide strap down her right shoulder, then her left. Next, she undid the zipper in the back, careful not to pull too hard when it caught in its usual place. She simply worked the fastener until it moved again.

A breeze from the ocean rolled by, sending a chill up her spine as she stepped out of the dress and let it fall to the ground. She wasn't completely naked, though. The gown was see-through at times, so she'd worn a nude-colored slip under it, the way she always had.

Her body shivered, and for a moment, she wondered if this was all wrong. If maybe, possibly, there was some way she could take it all back. See her daughters again. Hold them, feel them, love them. She could get dressed right now and just go home, forgetting this ever happened and revamping her search party efforts until they found the girls.

Her skin prickled at the thought, but then reality crashed back into her, nearly knocking her off her feet.

You were born to die young, remember, Emilia?

She clutched her stomach, letting the silent tears fall.

She hated that it had come to this.

Just then, a storm cloud thundered up ahead. It wasn't supposed to rain today, but then again, this was Cape Cod. The weather could change at a moment's notice, suicidal plans be damned.

Emilia looked up at the sky as a raindrop fell on her lip. And despite it all, she smiled. The drop tasted warm, like hot honey melting on your tongue at the end of a long day. She stretched her arms out wide and bent her head back, ready to drink up the sky's tears, the way she wished someone had drunk up hers over the last year. First, there was one, then two, then twelve drops, and within a few minutes, the previously sunny sky became a downpour, soaking Emilia through her slip.

"This seems fitting!" she yelled, keeping her arms cast wide as her hair became plastered to her face. Then, a laugh burst out of her. "I'm not even mad about it, whoever you are up there!"

She continued to giggle, her own tears intermingling with the clouds'. If this was going to be the last time she ever felt the rain on her skin, she was going to enjoy it.

Suddenly, she began to hum, a familiar song forming on her lips as she scooped up her last wine bottle.

"No one else can feel it . . ."

Another crack boomed overhead as she spun.

"No one else . . ."

She stopped twirling long enough to take a sip of the remaining *vino*, and then, in a final act of defiance, she tipped the bottle up further, drowning herself in a sea of fumes as the wine drizzled over her hair and skin.

Where your book begins . . .

Emilia picked up the hem of her slip and began to spin again, feeling the weight of it all: losing the girls, her brother's murder, the eclipse of her marriage. *Luca.* She spun and spun until she couldn't spin anymore, catching herself against a nearby tree.

Her fingers scraped against the bark as she tried to get her footing, but then, out of the corner of her eye, she saw a flash of purple.

Quick as lightning, she fell to the ground, striking it with her palms until she captured the tiny bellflowers. Dirt embedded itself under her nails, but she didn't care. More tears flowed freely from her face, a maniacal laughter consuming her.

Purple had always been her daughters' favorite color.

Her chest cracked as she clung to the tiny flowers, the sounds of the storm drowning out the wails of her agony. She lay there on the muddy earth as she cried and cried, denoting this as her final sign that they were gone. They had been killed, and now, they were ready to greet her in death.

Nothing about her story was unwritten. Her ending had been planned long ago, and now, it was time to execute the last chapter and finally discover what her epilogue held.

Wiping the snot from her nose and smearing dirt across her face in the process, Emilia finally stood as the rain began to mellow. She took the scoop of flowering plants, then walked around the edge of the cliff and collected more wildflowers, creating a bouquet fit for a sea burial.

NICK
NOW

MY BEAUTIFUL GIRLS.

Nick sat on the edge of Luella's hospital bed, hugging both of his daughters to his chest.

"I thought we'd never see you again," Tallulah whispered as tears slid down her face.

He kissed her forehead, squeezing them both a little tighter.

"I knew," Luella said, voice sassy and determined as ever. "I told you they'd find us, sissy."

Nick's heart cracked at their exchange, a smile consuming his face. They'd been sitting like this for several minutes, the essence of time and place ceasing to exist outside their small bubble. Nick had prayed for this moment so many times.

Thank you, Jesus.

A knock at the door sounded, forcing them all to open their eyes and glance over. Officer Holt, who'd previously been waiting outside the room, was now standing in the entryway with another man.

"Apologies for interrupting, but I have someone who I'd like you to meet, if that's okay."

Nick looked down at the girls, waiting for their permission. They each nodded but then clung closer to him, diverting their gazes and making Nick's heart constrict.

"Yes," he said after a moment. "Yes, come in."

Holt nodded, then stepped inside the room, allowing the other man in uniform to enter. "This is Special Agent Mark Rodriquez. He received intel from one of our informants that a transaction would be taking place early this morning. Rodriquez attended, having feigned interest in wanting to purchase a child. Once inside, he and his team were able to fully execute the rescue mission."

Nick appraised the man before him, taking in his stocky frame, tattoos, and tight-cropped haircut. He also didn't miss the way the girls flinched at his presence.

"Mr. Davenport," the agent said, extending his hand. "It's a pleasure to meet you."

Nick removed his arm from around Luella, accepting the man's warm gesture. He had so many things he wanted to say at this moment, so many things he wanted to ask. But that could wait until later because right now, the only thing he felt was gratitude.

"Thank you," he whispered, his voice already choking. "Thank you for bringing them home."

Rodriquez smiled softly, his eyes teary, too. "It was my pleasure, sir." He offered a curt nod, then turned his attention to Tallulah and Luella. "I know I looked scary in there, but thank you girls for trusting me when the time came. If it hadn't been for your bravery, we likely wouldn't have gotten out in time."

Shock registered through Nick's system yet again as he realized his daughters now shared a trauma bond with this man that he would never understand. He suddenly had a thousand more questions to ask. Were they really here in town all this time? Or were they brought back? How many disgusting, vile creatures had hurt his daughters? What will the recovery process look like? How can he protect them now, ensure this never happens again? The questions steamrolled through his brain. He was moments away from word vomiting them to the agent, but just as he parted his lips, Tallulah did something uncharacteristic.

She stood and gave the man a hug.

"Thank you," she cried, tightening her arms around his midsection. "Thank you for saving us from that hellhole."

"Careful, Tully," Luella said, nervously tucking a strand of hair behind her ear. "We're home now. Don't wanna get grounded for bad language on day one."

Nick, Rodriquez, and Holt all exchanged a glance before a gentle laughter permeated the room. Tallulah unwrapped herself from the agent and slid back on the bed next to Nick. "Shut up, Ellie. I knew I should've left you."

The energy in the room continued to shift as the joy crept in. They still had so much to do, so much to figure out, but for now, all was right in the world.

Until Luella's question.

"Where's Mom?"

"Yeah," Tallulah said, right on cue. "I wanna see her, and Luca."

Nick pulled out his phone then, having forgotten his concern with Emilia's whereabouts in the chaos of the moment. "I don't know," he said, thumbing to her messages. "I tried calling and texting her several times." He started to say something else, but the words fell off his tongue when he realized she had finally responded.

Emilia: *Goodbye. I love you, and I'm sorry. Please hug Luca for me.*

Nick
Now

"Dammit!"

Nick jumped from his spot on the bed, then quickly regretted it when Tallulah and Luella flinched.

"I'm so sorry, girls," he said. "Everything's fine, I just—"

His voice broke off, not finishing the thought as his mind jumbled, synapses firing in all the wrong places.

"What's wrong?" Holt asked.

Nick started to open his mouth again but then snapped it shut. How could he say the words he needed to say in front of his teenage daughters? And how was he supposed to leave them when he'd just gotten them back?

Not knowing what else to do, he slid his phone to the cop.

Officer Holt took it without hesitation, his gaze snapping quickly to the phone screen, then back to Nick. After a beat, he handed the device to Rodriquez, taking charge and formulating the plan Nick couldn't. "Girls, I need to borrow your father for some more questioning. Do you feel safe if I leave you in Rodriquez's care?"

Their eyes immediately grew wide.

"Is something wrong?" Tallulah asked.

"Yeah, please don't leave us yet, Daddy," Luella echoed.

Their words made Nick's throat dry up.

"No reason to be alarmed." Holt's face remained neutral, never once indicating that something was very much, in fact, wrong. "We just need to do some routine police work now that you're back in your parents' custody. I also believe the doctors would like to begin their examinations, but I know you both requested your mother's presence for that."

Examinations.

The word hit Nick's already gutted stomach that much harder. He looked to Luella, then Tallulah, noticing both of their cheeks reddening.

"Alright then," Holt said. "It's settled. We won't be long. And hopefully, we can find your mother for you while we're gone."

He nodded a quick thanks to Rodriguez before ushering Nick to the door.

"Wait," Nick said, throwing up his arms at the policeman. "I'm not—" A strangled sob took hold of his throat, the words sticking like honey. "I can't," he tried again. "I can't leave them. I just got them back."

He locked eyes on his daughters, and then all at once, as if pulled by a divine magnet, they all drew toward each other, messy limbs tangling until they were entirely intertwined. His body ached as he heard their muffled sobs. What was he thinking? There was no way he could leave them.

Emilia's on the edge of a fucking cliff right now.

A hand grabbed his shoulder for the second time today, pulling slightly. "Come on, Nick," Holt said. "They'll be safe."

"One hundred percent," Rodriquez said. "I give you my word."

Nick looked between the two men, fear and urgency coating his veins. His daughters had just been delivered home to him after an entire year of horrifying trauma, and now he had to go gallivanting off to save his wife from killing herself?

And here he thought this was going to be the best day of his life.

Let's go, Holt mouthed, and after a moment, Nick nodded.

"Okay," he said, clearing his throat and stifling the remaining tears. "Girls, I promise you, I will be right back in just a few hours. I promise, you are completely safe here." He looked from Tully to Ellie, wanting more than anything to take away their pain. "No one, and I mean *no one*, is ever going to hurt you again."

For a moment, no one said anything. It was dead silent in the room as everyone waited on bated breath to see what would happen next, and then, Tallulah said, "Pinky promise?"

Nick let out a monstrous breath, his chest tightening into a feeling that hurt so good it ached. "Pinky promise."

The girls nodded, and with that, Nick kissed them both on the forehead one last time, then followed Officer Holt out the door, down the elevator, and into the police car.

"Where to?" Holt slammed his door and turned on his flashing lights.

"Fiore Vineyards," Nick said without hesitation.

Because there was only one place Emilia would go to die.

"DID YOU KNOW SHE was suicidal?" Holt asked as he rounded the corner on Main Street.

Nick chewed his lip. "I don't know. I mean, maybe on some level." He ducked his head, checking the street ahead as his legs bounced in his seat. "She hasn't handled any of this well, but then again, neither have I, and I'm not contemplating offing myself. We have a son, for crying out loud!"

Thinking about Luca touched a raw nerve deep inside him. If Emilia was in pain, fine. If she had depression, okay, lots of people did. If she had needed help, he would've gotten her help. He would've done anything under the sun for that woman, especially with the absence of the twins. But what he would not do, could not do, was forgive her if she voluntarily left their son. Leaving him was one thing, but their child? Luca was only six. He still needed his mother.

Anger raged beneath his skin. He needed a distraction. Deciding to call her again, he pulled out his phone and pressed the photo of them at their wedding, wondering how in the hell they'd gone from that beautiful, whimsical moment to the harsh reality they lived in now. Seconds ticked by as he waited for the line to ring, but of course, it didn't. His call went straight to voicemail, just like all the others had.

"Dammit," he hissed again under his breath.

"Almost there." Holt turned on his blinker, speeding past a blur of staring faces. "How long ago did she send the text?"

Nick glanced back at his phone, mentally calculating the time. "Twenty minutes ago."

Holt pushed his foot down on the gas pedal, revving the engine in response.

"If you go in the back way, you can loop around to the edge of the woods. That'll be quicker."

The officer nodded, checking his mirrors before making a sharp left turn.

"Just over there," Nick said, pointing toward the hidden driveway. "Behind the honeysuckle bushes."

Holt steered the car onto the gravel road along the back edge of Fiore Vineyards, spraying rocks everywhere as he skittered toward the gate. Nick unbuckled his seat belt and emerged from the car before it had even fully stopped, falling in the process. He rolled to his knees, then pushed himself off the ground and ran toward the gate, prying it open as quickly as he could, rust flakes from the weathered bar rubbing into his palms.

At last, the gate gave, and Nick shoved it open. He tore through the muddy terrain, evidence of the storm that just rolled through splashing against his skin. He didn't care, though. He would ruin all of his clothes, throw them all into the sea and set them on fire, if it meant getting to her in time.

His *amore*.

He would spend every minute of every day hating her and loving her all the same if he could just save her, stop her from this volitional act that would forever ruin their family.

At last, he jumped over the final tree trunk at the forest's edge, indicating he was close to the cliff. He could see the tops of the lavender fields and grapevines lining the outskirts of the winery, and there, just on the edge of the horizon, was his Italian beauty.

His heart skipped a beat, and he nearly tripped as he saw her long black hair blowing in the wind.

"Emilia!" he yelled, praying desperately that the same wind would carry his voice to her. "Emilia! Don't jump!"

He broke through the clearing, and now he could see all of her. She was dressed in nothing but a nude slip, which clung to her curves. Her hair was wet, no doubt from the rain, and she was standing on the very edge of the cliff, one foot floating above the air, the other barely holding her in place.

"Emilia! Don't—"

EMILIA
NOW

EMILIA DANGLED HER FOOT over the ledge, slowly raising her arms for balance.

That's it, Emilia. Just jump.

Tears streamed down her face as she took in the last few breaths she ever would. In a moment, this world would fall away, and she would cross over to whatever was next.

Deep down, in the pit of her stomach, she hoped it was Heaven, or at least, something like that. But that's the thing about hope. It lets you down too easily. It's a dangerous flame that can be extinguished all too quickly, but not before searing the edges of your heart, blackening your soul.

That's what color Emilia imagined hers was.

Waves crashed below her, some angry, others soothing, as if they couldn't decide whether they were vengeful or sympathetic.

Not that she deserved either reaction.

She deserved nothing at all for the sins she'd committed.

It's time.

The voice seethed under her skull, and she nodded, inhaling one last breath.

"I'm so sorry, girls," she whispered. "You—"

"Emilia! Don't jump!"

Shock rang through her system at the sound of her husband's voice, and she turned her head, tears obstructing her vision.

But after blinking a few times, she realized no one was there.

Had she imagined it? Was this all one last cruel joke to punctuate her time—

"Emilia! Don't—oh my God, don't jump!"

But then she heard it again, and this time, the familiar shape of her husband appeared. The sight of him was enough to instantly crush her.

Turn away. Jump now. Ignore him.

"Go away, Nick!" she cried as she looked back at the sea, her voice catching in her throat. "You weren't supposed to see this." It was a shallow attempt to shield him from this one last tragedy.

"Emilia, they found them!"

She snapped her head to the side, daring another angled glance at her husband.

"The girls, Emmy! They found the girls."

Jump!

But she ignored the chaos in her mind, that fleeting feeling of hope once again rising in her chest.

It's not true, the voice said. *He's lying to keep you from doing this.*

But Nick wouldn't lie to her about this, would he? Even with her on the brink of death, he would know better than to tell her a falsehood as great as this one, which must mean—

"They're at West General Hospital." He was closer now, nearly behind her. "Please, Emmy. Our daughters are home. They're safe."

At that, her world broke around her, the shattering fragments of her living nightmare turning into a new awakening. "They're...home?" she asked quietly, weighing the words on her tongue, seeing if they'd hold or shove her off this mountain.

"Yes," Nick said, his voice still urgent but more gentle. "Please, step away from the ledge, and come see them with me."

"They're home," Emilia repeated to herself. She looked down at her foot as it hovered over the ledge, seeing how close she'd come to death.

And then she couldn't help herself.

She laughed.

A joyous, off-pitch yet still harmonious laugh rang from her lips, and she pivoted around on the heel of her balanced foot, hope now flooding her chest.

"My babies—"

An unsteadiness wavered beneath her, cutting off her words.

No.

"Emilia!"

Another panicked sensation overwhelmed her, seizing her lungs. Because at that very moment, Emilia slipped, losing her footing and her balance with it.

"Nick!" she screamed as her body skimmed down the side of the rock face. "Nick, help me!"

She tried digging her nails into the rock, desperately trying to get a grip, but it was no use. In an instant, she had already fallen too much, too far away for Nick to reach her, even if he tried.

This was it.

This was how Emilia was going to die.

Young, just like she'd always predicted.

"Emmy!"

Nick's voice was frantic in the background, but the fear inside Emilia's chest had already resolved to dust. Soon, she would splatter against the rocks, the execution of her original plan finally fulfilled.

In a way, it was comforting.

Because despite having one last fighting notion to live, she was at peace with the world.

Because her daughters were alive.

There is a God.

Despite what she'd done, despite what they'd been through, they were alive.

And they were home.

Safe.

He's real.

Emilia looked up, capturing one final image of her husband as the clouds rolled away, the warmth of the sunshine spreading across her skin.

Then, she fell to her final demise, praying the Lord would use these tides to wash away her sins.

It was death by baptism, death by life, all in the same notion.

EMILIA

THEN

"Where are the girls?"

Emilia directed the question at Nick as he carried a sleeping Luca in his arms.

"Still at the bonfire with some friends." He shifted his son's head to the side before continuing. "I spoke to Cass. He's gonna bring them home for us so we can get Luca in bed."

Nodding, Emilia smoothed a hand over her son's messy hair. "Sweet boy," she whispered. "He's had a long day."

Nick nodded, stifling a yawn in the process. "You ready?"

Instead of responding right away, Emilia turned, pivoting her gaze to the remaining guests. The summer solstice party had ended half an hour ago, but a handful of people still remained. Emilia could see at least a dozen locals scattered throughout the grounds, along with a few employees who'd clocked out and were having a drink. She should really stay until everyone was gone, but she knew Nick wanted her to come home with him.

"Yes," she said slowly, turning back to Nick. "I just need to make sure Zoey can stay until everyone's gone. You boys go on. I'll be right behind you."

Nick wrinkled his brow. "You sure?"

She nodded quickly, then smiled. "Yes, go on. Put little man to sleep, and I'll be home shortly."

With a quick peck, they said their goodbyes, and Emilia promised not to stay out too late.

"I'm serious," Nick said as he walked away. "No more work. Come home to me, *amore mio*."

Her skin tingled at the promise of what was to come. "Don't worry, darling. I'm just going to touch base with Zo, then I'll be home." She blew him another kiss, then looked back at the winery.

It was just after eleven, and despite the festivities being officially over, the energy in the air was vibrant, calculated. Like everyone who remained knew this would be a permanent memory seared into their brain for the rest of time.

Emilia shuddered, noting the slow rise of goose bumps on her arms. The mist from the sea had started to roll in, creating an ethereal fog over the vineyard. Everywhere she looked, guests and fires and lights were coated by plumes of hazy summer fog, and Emilia swore she could detect a hint of rain in the air.

She didn't see Zoey amongst the crowd, but Emilia could almost guarantee she was inside, hiding from Cass's advances. Chasing the goose bumps away, Emilia rubbed her arms and slipped off her heels, then started walking toward the office. She remembered stuffing a jacket in the supply closet earlier that morning, so hopefully, she could kill two birds with one stone on this visit.

Moments later, she stepped inside the admin building, careful to wipe her feet off before padding across the cool tile.

"Zoey?" she called as she made her way through the small lobby.

Outside, a large outburst of giggles sounded, and Emilia paused, ducking her head to look out the nearby window. The bonfire had exploded to double its size, illuminating the happy faces of her twins and a few of their friends. She felt an inherent need to scold them, to warn them about fire safety, but seeing them there, twirling by the firelight and not having a care in the world—well, it made her smile.

She removed her fingers from the window sill, calling Zoey's name again several times as she wandered past the open employee workspace, then the kitchen.

Hmm.

Maybe she was outside after all.

Emilia still needed her jacket, though, so she resumed her journey to the supply closet, crossing her fingers none of the staff members had snagged it. It was both a blessing and a curse to have a team that felt like family.

"There you are," she mumbled as she swung the door open and saw the brown pleather garment hanging inside.

"And there you are."

The words sent a chill down her rigid spine, and Emilia stilled, hand frozen in midair.

"Oh, come on," the voice continued, "don't be shy. We were just getting to know you."

Emilia felt the cold barrel of a gun sting the back of her neck, and she spoke quickly, acting on impulse. "The money's in the safe."

The man sneered, his voice gravelly and low. "It's a little too late for that, sweetheart. We're way past pleasantries at this point."

He pressed the cool barrel further into her skin, and Emilia's heart stuttered. In all her years on the vineyard, they'd never once been robbed, let alone held at gunpoint. The severity of the situation made her stomach drop.

"What do you want?" She was trying to be brave, but her voice came out small and weak.

Suddenly, the gun disappeared from her back, and she slumped her shoulders, letting out a huge sigh of relief as sweat pooled under her arms.

"What do I want?" The man laughed. "Well, I think that's a question you should ask *him*."

Emilia was still facing the closet, so she had no idea who the man was referring to. All she knew was that her heart was thundering so loudly, so rapidly in her chest, she could barely hear herself think.

"Let's go, doll." The man grabbed her hair and then yanked her away from the closet. "I think you're really going to like this part."

She nearly tripped as the man led her down the hallway and into her office, panic and bile rising simultaneously in her throat. As they moved, she felt disconnected from her body, like this wasn't really happening to her and she was merely watching it happen to someone else.

Except it was happening to her.

Someone was nearly ripping her hair out of her skull and shoving her down the hallway, all with the threat of a loaded gun.

Only when they got to her office did the reality set in, crashing into her like a monsoon.

Cass.

When they reached the door, Emilia's eyes grew wide as she took in the sight. Her brother sitting on his knees, bound and gagged. Bruises swelling over his eye sockets. His blood splattered on the floor. Two other terrifying men pointing equally terrifying guns at him. It was like a scene from a horror movie.

"Go on," the man said, shoving her inside.

She staggered before falling beside her brother. When he looked at her, his eyes were wild with something crazed and apologetic that Emilia didn't yet understand.

What have you done, Cass?

The man who'd shoved her cleared his throat, although it did nothing to make his tone sound less rough. Emilia flicked her gaze to him, taking in his appearance for the first time. He was smaller than she'd imagined. Less than six feet and too thin to be able to manhandle her the way he had. He was nearly bald, and his skin was tan, a smattering of freckles highlighting his cheeks. If it weren't for the neck tattoos, he'd almost look normal.

Harmless.

"Alright, princess," he started, admiring his weapon. "Why don't you ask your precious brother what it is we want."

Emilia looked from the man to Cass, then to the two bouncers in the room, who, she noted, looked much more like typical criminals.

"I said *ask!*"

She nearly peed herself from the sudden inflection, fear consuming her. "What do they want, Cassio?"

The man nodded to one of the other two, who then ripped off the duct tape from Cassio's mouth. He screamed, then took a moment to steady his breathing.

"You better answer the little lady."

Cassio's voice was strained, but he answered none the same. "I don't know."

Using the back of his gun, the man struck a blow to Cassio's face, leaving an immediate bruise. Emilia screamed, and Cass bent over, coughing blood on the floor.

"Roland," one of the other two warned.

Roland rolled in his lips, anger seething as Emilia's fear continued to climb. "I'm sorry, boys." He paused, shifting his gaze to Emilia. "Boss man doesn't like it when we get our hands too dirty. DNA gets messy, you see. But when someone pisses me off, I don't know. Sometimes I just find it hard to control myself."

Emilia still had no idea what was happening, why these men were here, or what her brother had to do with any of it. What she did know was that her daughters were just outside and could come in any minute. She had to ensure that didn't happen.

"Please," she whimpered. "Please, just tell me what you want. I told you, all our money's in the safe. I can give you the code—"

Roland cut her off. "Ticktock, ticktock, *amico*. You better start speaking soon before I have to tell your dear old sister what you did."

"I don't know what he's talking about," Cassio said to Emilia, still panting from his spot on the floor.

Roland laughed again. "Now see, that's where you're wrong, my friend." He pulled out a small device from his pocket and made a show of attaching it to his gun. Emilia's eyes grew as she registered the silencer. "Your lies are really starting to piss me off."

"I swear," Cassio cried, but again Roland cut him off, this time by shoving the gun into Emilia's temple, sending a wave of pure terror throughout every inch of her skin. "No!" he screamed. "Please, please don't hurt her."

"Confess or sissy gets a bullet in the head."

Silent tears ran down Emilia's face as she wondered what her brother could've possibly done to initiate all of this.

"Okay," Cass said, panic still evident in his voice. "Okay, I-I stole money from the ring. I skimmed, just a little, from the top, hoping you wouldn't notice."

And suddenly, it all made sense. The sudden influx of cash, the frequent visits, the shady phone calls. She'd known for a while something was going on with Cassio, but she'd never imagined it would be this.

"And there it is." Roland removed the gun from Emilia's line of vision, and her heart sank yet again. "Cassio stole from us. And do you know what happens to those who steal from people like us, Emilia?"

She didn't need to answer.

"Do you know what happens when you try to rip off the world's most powerful sex trafficking ring?"

Sex trafficking.

Emilia's ears went deaf at the words.

"No," Cassio pleaded. "Please. I'm sorry."

Roland cracked his head to the side, eyes locking on Emilia. "It's too late for that, buddy. You should've thought of that before you did what you did. The boss isn't happy about this."

Emilia's mind was blank, her ears still ringing with shock.

Surely, she'd heard him wrong.

"Please," Cassio continued. "Please, don't hurt her. It was my mistake. Just kill me, and let her go."

"Mmm," Roland said, walking in small circles around the room. "If only it were that simple." He stopped pacing long enough to shift his gaze to a photo on the wall.

And that's when Emilia's life flipped upside down.

"You see, we don't want her. No offense, Emmy, but you're too old for our clientele." He took another step toward the family portrait she'd hung last spring, and fresh tears sprang to her eyes. "We work with youth. Call it a specialty service."

"No!" Cassio shouted, sitting back up on his knees. "Absolutely not. You are not allowed to touch them. That was part of our deal when I got involved with Ferdinand. I helped you clean your cash and cook the books, and no one, not a single soul, could touch my family."

Emilia's jaw dropped at hearing this new information.

Roland shook his head, a sinister smile playing on his lips before he shot his gaze to his two goons. "Isn't it funny, boys, how he thinks he has a say in this?"

The other men laughed, echoing his sentiment, while Cassio continued to argue.

"No, please, I'm the one who fucked up." He looked from Roland to the two men before his gaze finally settled on Emilia. "Please," he whispered, and then, "I'm so sorry, Emmy. I never meant—"

A loud bang sounded, and Emilia jumped as she watched the life drain out of her brother. His gaze widened slightly, and then, all at once, he fell to the ground, a pool of blood quickly spreading.

"The boss isn't going to like that." Roland tsked, then apologized to his associates. "Sorry, boys. I'll handle the cleanup."

The men continued to grunt in the background, but Emilia was frozen, both in time and space. From the moment the bullet hit Cassio's chest to the second he crashed on the tiled floor, his blood pouring out, had felt like both an eternity and no time at all. Simply a blip on her radar that would forever change the trajectory of her life.

"Now," Roland said, interrupting her thoughts. "Where were we?"

Too stunned to speak, Emilia simply lifted her eyes from her brother's dead body to greet the face of a monster.

"As I was saying, unfortunately, since brother dearest here voided our contract, it's time we collect due payment, plus interest." He swiveled back to the portrait on the wall and pointed at the children, shocking Emilia back to her senses.

"No," she said once, low and firm, then again, louder and with more conviction. "No. You can have me, but do not touch my children."

Roland blew out an exasperated breath. "Emilia, Emilia, we've been over this. You're too old, baby. I mean, don't get me wrong, you're beautiful. I would love to have my way with you if it were up to me, but as I said, our clients prefer a younger demographic."

Emilia wasn't giving up. "No. Cassio is the one who screwed you over, not us. Take someone else's kids if you must, but not mine. Do *not* take mine."

The earlier fear and shock she'd felt had transformed into a dire desperation to save her children, to do whatever necessary to protect them from this evil. Venom dripped from her lips at the idea of these men, any man, touching her sweet children.

She wouldn't allow it.

Roland held her gaze for a moment, then flicked his eyes to the other men. "I don't think she's understanding, boys."

Then, without warning, the man to Emilia's left yanked her upward before slamming her body onto the desk. Emilia cried involuntarily as the man then yanked her underwear down and hiked up her dress, exposing her bare ass to the cold and everyone in the room. Instantly, her body froze, taking her back to that awful night twenty years ago when a stranger had committed a similar act.

Taken advantage of her body without her permission, taking her independence and youth with it. She'd never told anyone, hopeful the core memory would lie dormant in the recesses of her thoughts.

She heard the familiar sound of a zipper, and her chest constricted as she lay there, holding Roland's gaze as he allowed his associate to make a show of her. She was biting the inside of her lip, waiting for the inevitable, when Roland crouched down to her level and held up a hand.

"We can do this the easy way, or the hard way." His face was close enough for her to spit in. "One way or another, your family owes us, and we intend to collect." He searched her face, finding only venom and froth. "And because I'm not a heartless man, tonight, I'm giving you a choice. The girls or the boy. Which will it be?"

Emilia didn't even breathe before responding. "Neither. Ever."

Roland clenched his jaw, nodded, then looked away. "I guess we're doing this the hard way."

The sound of jeans hitting the floor echoed in the quiet of the tiny room, and Emilia winced. Before she even had time to process what was happening, the man who'd pinned her down shoved himself inside her, eliciting an involuntary scream. Her body burned and raged all over as she tried to reject him, but after one pump, his advances continued until his body stilled at Roland's demand.

"Now just imagine if this were your daughters," he said, a lifeless strain in his voice. "Do you think they'd enjoy it more or less than your son?"

Then, without warning, the man behind her shoved himself inside Emilia's back entrance, causing her to scream and cry as he defiled her body. The pain was excruciating, but it was nothing compared to the white-hot shame she felt burning inside her lungs.

"I don't know about you, but I think it might be a little more traumatizing for the little one."

"You're disgusting!" she screamed as the man behind her once again shoved himself inside her asshole, taking everything, and nothing, from her.

Roland licked his lips, stroking a piece of hair that had fallen across Emilia's face. "We can do this all night until you make a choice." He paused, brushing her lips with his thumb. "As I said, I'd love to have my way with you."

"You could rape me for the rest of eternity, and I would still never choose." She held his gaze, emphasizing her truth.

She would go to the ends of the earth to protect her children from these pedophiles.

After a moment, Roland nodded, a new light shining in his eyes. "Okay then, little mamma. How 'bout this? Either you pick who you'd like to hand over to us, or we kill all three?"

The remaining life was zapped out of her at those words.

"No," she rasped. "No, you can't. Please—"

Her voice broke, and Roland feigned innocence. "'No, no, please, you can't hurt my babies.'" He laughed at his own joke before standing. "I assure you, I can, and I will. This is just business."

He snapped his fingers, and the man who'd been raping her zipped himself back up. Roland yanked Emilia by the hair again, pulling her to a seated position, her lower half still exposed. "Now, I'm going to ask you one last time before I walk out there and shoot Tallulah and Luella in the chest, then drive to your home and kill Luca and your sweet husband, too, while I'm at it."

No, Emilia silently begged as he pulled harder on her hair, saltwater tears drowning her face. "Please."

She was at a loss for words.

Roland smirked, delighting in her torment. "And let's say, for added measure, that if you do choose but then leave and tell someone about what transpired here tonight, I'll personally come back and kill whomever you saved."

No, no, no.

Emilia felt like she was drowning, his words waterboarding her soul.

Roland lowered his head, meeting her gaze. Their eyes remained locked as the seconds ticked by, until finally, he whispered the words she'd been dreading.

"Who do you choose?"

THE END

*If you are experiencing suicidal thoughts, please call or text **988** for immediate help.*

ACKNOWLEDGEMENTS

I am in awe that I've reached the end of another book. Although this is only a novella, it feels like the most powerful story I've written. It's certainly my favorite.

As with any book, though, I had several wonderful people helping behind the scenes.

To Briana, my amazing editor, thank you so much for tackling this project! It was a delight working together, and I'll forever be grateful for your keen eye and attention to detail. BRB while I sing your praises to the masses.

To Mel, my brilliant cover designer, *thank you* for bringing my vision to life! I could cry from how much I love this beautiful cover.

To Haley, Rachel, and Madi, my alpha readers, thank you for braving the roughest version of this story. You three are gems, and I'm so grateful for your friendship and support. Emilia's demise wouldn't be the same without your input.

To Michael, the real-life Officer Holt, thank you for ensuring the police procedural aspects of this story were accurate. A Starbucks pink drink is coming your way.

To Danielle, Taylor, and Christina, my beta readers, thank you so much for being my last line of defense before this went to my editor. I so value your time and input, and those hype comments were a special kind of love.

To Alexis, my author bestie, thank you for listening to me talk about this story nonstop. You know I couldn't do this without you! (Now shut the book and go write!)

To Jessica Renee Ryan, my kick-ass audiobook narrator, thank you SO MUCH for taking a chance on this story and bringing my characters to life. Bless the clock app for bringing us together!

To Seth, my sweet husband, thank you for everything you do for our family. Because of you, I get to raise our babies and live out my dream of being an author. You'll never know how much that means; I feel truly blessed to have you as my partner.

To Willow and Ezra, my beautiful babies, thank you so much for just being you. I love you both so much, and I hope you know I would never choose. Emilia's story is quite literally my worst nightmare. I pray for your divine protection every day.

To my family, thank you all for your amazing support. I love how much you believe in me and these demented stories. And a special shoutout to my mom for always keeping me safe while growing up, even when I was a brat.

Lastly, to the ladies in my Bible study group last spring, thank you for putting up with my morbid fascination with Jeffrey Dahmer and his salvation. Your willingness to openly discuss this concept largely prompted the spiritual aspect of this story, so thank you. I only hope I did it justice.

YOU'RE INVITED
Summer Solstice
VINO
party
INTRODUCING:
Lavanda
BLANC
FRIDAY, JUNE 20 | 7 PM
FIORE VINEYARDS

READY FOR MORE DISTURBINGLY SHOCKING PLOT TWISTS?

Check out this exclusive sneak peek from SECRET SANTA, a psychological Christmas thriller releasing this fall.

ISLA
NOW

The sharp edges of the coffin reflected in Isla's gaze.

Breathe.

Not exactly how she'd planned to kick off the holidays, especially as a business owner, yet here she was, standing inside the oversized sanctuary of a massive Catholic church in her hometown of Wilderby, West Virginia, staring at her ex-best friend's casket.

It'd been three days since she got the call about Rebecca's death. She'd been standing in the storage closet at her coffee shop, attempting to carry way too many bags of flour, and had dropped them all, coating herself and the room in a sea of white dust. *Head injury, freak accident, subdural hematoma, nothing they could do.* The memories played on repeat as she took another step now, wondering how long Rebecca had been dead, lying there on the basement floor of her house before her roommate found her.

The line moved, and Isla shuddered, trying to expunge the thought. She took a steadying breath and prepared herself for what was next. She'd been to several funerals before, but they were always for older people—grandparents, great aunts, a friendly neighbor. She'd never seen the dead body of someone her own age, much less someone so close to her.

Someone she considered a friend, a soul sister. *A source of trauma.*

A man behind Isla coughed, and she knew that was her cue to move, to step forward and visit the front of the casket, *paying her respects*. The thought sent a rigid chill down her spine, causing her skin to tingle.

You can do this.

You have *to do this.*

Nodding, she walked toward the midnight-colored coffin, fear stabbing in her throat. Slowly, Rebecca's body came into view, and Isla shuddered. Becca had always been thin due to both genetics and an eating disorder, but the mere skeletal figure lying inside the satin-lined box was almost unrecognizable.

Sweet Becca, she thought. *You deserved so much more.*

Digging her nails into the palms of her hands, Isla trailed her gaze up Rebecca's corpse, skimming over her auburn hair and landing on her face. Isla took in Becca's swollen eye sockets, busted lips, and ruptured varicose veins, all while a thunderous crack vibrated in her chest. She couldn't comprehend why Becca's parents had opted for an open casket ceremony when she looked like this.

Unable to stare at this version of her old friend any longer, Isla cleared her throat and blew a kiss, letting the gesture melt away into an "I love you" sign. Her heart squeezed as she realized Rebecca wasn't going to wake up and return their signature signal, so Isla swallowed the lump in her throat and flew past the receiving line. She reached one of the wooden pews in the center of the room and settled into an empty spot.

Deep breaths, Isla.

Needing a distraction, she cast a glance at the other guests. Although she hadn't lived in Wilderby for nearly a decade, Isla recognized several faces. Mr. Joss, their high school English teacher, stood at the front of the line, flanked by an onslaught of other faculty members. Next was Darcy Jones, owner of Thick Chicks, the town's go-to bar and restaurant—and coincidentally, the place where Rebecca worked until her death. Even at thirty-one, she was still slinging beers to country bumpkins and wannabe lumberjacks.

Trailer trash, her mind whispered.

Isla's skin prickled as shame encompassed her. Because that's what they'd called Becca when they were younger. And sometimes when they were older, depending on the mood.

Isla crossed one leg over the other, clasping her hands over her lap and adjusting the black lace hem of her skirt. She didn't want to think about that today.

Ignoring the guilt that lined the pit of her stomach, she resumed her scan of the other faces in the audience, and that's when she saw the first living member of her old friend group.

Her heartbeat sped tenfold as Wren Jenkins tossed her long, honey-blonde hair behind her shoulder before dabbing her eyes with a napkin and then letting her hand fall to her stomach. Isla watched Wren make circles around the bump, and her chest tightened. Everything had always come so naturally for Wren. Marriage, motherhood, health, wellness. Hell, even now, Wren's body looked immaculate, even after four kids and another on the way. She was like a golden fertility goddess, a stark contrast to Isla's childless loins and dark, gothic appearance. She'd always felt incomparable to Mother Hen Wren.

Envy started to creep up her vertebrae, one by one, but before the feeling could settle too deep, she felt a sweep of cool air move by. Stiffening against the rough grain of the pew, she turned to the side, heart palpitating like a racehorse. This wasn't the time or the—

"I can't believe you're wearing a hat inside a church."

Liam.

Isla's shoulders relaxed at the sound of his voice.

"I didn't think you were going to be here," she whispered, tipping her black straw hat to the side so she could hug her favorite member of their former clique. "You said you'd be in New York until the end of the month."

Liam released her grip and settled into the pew beside her. "Change of plans. There was no way I was going to miss this."

Isla smiled at his response, a lightness she didn't know she needed pulling inside her chest; she'd missed him more than she realized. Liam, Rebecca, and Isla had been the tightest-knit trio in their group after the pair had absorbed Isla into their world. Liam and Rebecca were the type of people who just paired naturally based on chemistry, an instant connection that only true best friends could share as they delighted in each other's orbit. Isla, on the other hand, had simply been a speckle of lone stardust, floating near their trajectory until gravity sucked her into their path.

If only they'd stayed the course and not burned out, yearning for the brightness of the sun, the complexity of the stars around them, then maybe Rebecca would still be alive.

"Have you seen the others yet?"

Isla startled at Liam's voice again, and she straightened in her seat. "Wren's up there." She paused to nod at the line and waited for Liam's gaze to follow. "I don't know about Scarlett or Carley."

Liam huffed out a laugh. "Oh, you know Scar is never far behind Wren. Those two are still attached at the hip."

Isla smirked, knowing he was right. Scarlett and Wren were another duo the universe could never seem to tear apart. Their bond was stronger than gravity, constantly pulling them back together. Isla used to find it odd that someone as loving and nurturing as Wren gravitated toward a person like Scarlett, an artificial queen bee, but over the years, she realized Wren was just as devious. She was just better at hiding it.

"I saw Carley was in Paraguay last week," Isla whispered, shifting her thoughts. She pulled out her phone to check their other friend's Instagram account, where she was once again startled at the thirty-six-million-count following. No one expected Carley's camping vlog to take off the way it did after she dropped out of college junior year. Isla and the rest of their crew had been nasty, cruel even, the way they made fun of her behind her back. Joke's on them now, though, Isla supposed, as Carley was the one living the dream. "If she's off the grid, she may not even know about Bec."

Liam nodded, his gaze drifting back to the line.

"Have you been up there, to see her?" Isla asked after a beat of silence.

He shook his head. "No. Don't want to remember her that way." He paused, raking his fingers through his ashy brown hair, dismantling the carefully gelled spikes. "I'm not good with death, not since—"

Isla's heart squeezed as Liam's voice trailed off, tears forming around his golden irises. It'd been almost two years since Liam lost his little brother, Trey, in a tragic car accident. Since then, he'd been coping by burying his head in the sand and working ridiculous hours at his start-up firm in New York City. He seldom talked about Trey, and Isla was ashamed to admit she sometimes forgot Liam had a brother.

Another ghost of their past, ready and willing to haunt them.

Just like Rebecca will.

Isla shifted in her seat again, shaking away the thought and giving Liam's hand a light squeeze. "It's okay," she said. "Bec would understand."

Isla felt a small tug back, and then the hum of an old, familiar hymn began buzzing from the front. Suddenly, the crowd caught a rift, a harmonious acapella version of "I'll Fly Away" humming through the air and echoing down the church corridor as everyone sang.

Fly away, Rebecca, Isla thought between each verse. *Fly away from this forsaken place.*